MIDNIGHT COURT

An Urban Fantasy

ANN GIMPEL

CONTENTS

MIDNIGHT COURT

MAGICK AND MISFITS SERIES, BOOK TWO

An Urban Fantasy

By

Ann Gimpel

**Tumble off reality's edge into a twisted world
fueled by myth and magick**

Copyright Page

Urban fantasy and slow burn romance wrapped into a serial that will keep you up reading long into the night.

Strange bedfellows rock worlds.

My days as Faery's reluctant regent have crashed and burned. Either I left the land to rot in a squalid soup of broken promises, or I destroyed her enemies one by one. No choice there. Not really. I'd known some of those "enemies" since childhood, which was centuries ago. They say familiarity breeds contempt. In my case it bred sorrow as I consigned Fae who'd been friends to eternal destruction and fed them to the land.

Dariyah, the Witch-who-wasn't-one, crossed my path for reasons I'm still figuring out. Her long-lost mother presided over one of Faery's many dirty secrets, the Midnight Court. Some like to believe Fae blood is pure. It's not. We and the Sidhe are joined at the hip, and the Midnight Court was once a living symbol of our bond.

I'll fight to maintain a magical world that's open to all. If I'm quick, ruthless, I might beat Oberon at his own game. Sly bastard that he is, he still holds the link to Faery. If I can't wrest it from him, the land—my land—will wither and fade.

AUTHOR'S NOTE

Book covers play a big role in my creative process. I saw a set of covers featuring a badass Fae prince a while back and bid on them. Unfortunately, someone had a faster Internet connection than me, so I didn't end up with them. But everything comes out as it should because I found another cover I liked even better: the one on *Court of Rogues*, first of the Magick and Misfits books.

I've always been fascinated with the Otherworld. The faeries' ancestral home goes by many names. It's called *Annwn* in Welsh mythology and *Avalon* in Arthurian legend. In Irish mythology it's referred to as *Tír na nÓg, Mag Mell,* and *Emain Ablach*. Irish myths also feature a place called *Tech Duinn*, where the souls of the dead gather.

But I digress. My vision is a world where mortal and faery collide.

You, my readers, will let me know how well I managed it.

PROLOGUE, AURIL

Auril clung to patterns, to sameness. She had little choice; consistency made the impossible bearable. For the first couple of centuries, she'd kept track of time passing, but it was depressing. So many days, weeks, years had dripped past, time no longer mattered. This wasn't like prison because it never ended. And it sure as hell wasn't anything like the *Dreaming,* a retreat anticipating your every whim. No *Dreaming* for her. Not ever. She'd always viewed herself as a loner, self-contained. Until she was faced with endless isolation. Then she realized she'd been deluding herself all along.

Once she'd been the Queen of Air and Darkness. But a queen requires subjects, and they were no more. She'd moved on, leaving the shell of queendom behind, the court she'd presided over erased by absence and the passage of centuries.

Too late to do anything about it. It had been too late for an exceedingly long while. Besides, it wasn't as if she'd had options. Not really. By the time she'd stumbled onto this world hidden from all others, the dice were tossed. No going back. She had a toddler to raise. Young as Dariyah was, power shimmered around her like a veil, spilling from her hair, her eyes, her fingertips in an endless stream of possibilities.

The child was beauty incarnate, with a sweet and inquisitive soul. Bright, curious, inspired, she more than made up for everything Auril had left behind. She'd seen some of the future unfold in her glass. More in various pools. Regardless, she'd viewed enough to understand her child was a critical element, an instrument meant to shape the future.

Her sister, Titania, wasn't one to put much stock in prophecies. She'd talked until no more words came, urging Auril to look past the life that had taken root in her womb. Many magic-wielders had walked in her foot-steps, had taken measures to deal with mixed-breed offspring. Those had been Titania's words: deal with it. Innocuous enough, except in this instance dealing meant death. Auril couldn't have done that any more than she could have cut off an arm or a leg. The child was destined to be. Its call from the beyond—an amorphous spot where souls resided—was so strong, it had swept her up in its urgency.

And so she'd fled from both Fae and Sidhe, from her duties to the Midnight Court, knowing there'd be fallout. And there had been. Her energy was a lynchpin keeping Faery whole. Between her and her sister, they'd balanced the dark and light sides of magic, feeding Faery and keeping her hale and hearty.

She'd asked questions a million different ways, working to tease out if her worst fears for Faery had come to pass. No answers had been forthcoming until a few days ago when a scrying attempt blew up in her face, showering her with water and leaving her with a deeply uncomfortable premonition the world she'd abandoned was finally unraveling at the seams.

Auril wrapped her arms around her bent knees and slumped against the rocky wall behind her. Should she return? After all this time, no one would remember the whispered rumors about a forbidden pregnancy. Eh, the ancient librarian, Ysir, might, but he'd been well on his way to madness long before she left.

Obscuring the relationship between Fae and Sidhe was another dirty little secret she'd been part of. The two lines sprang from common roots, and their power blended perfectly, creating awe-inspiring magic. Remembering its perfection still stole her breath. The multi-hued strands of talent had filled her with joy as they knitted into various spells. The same blended power terrified Oberon, perhaps because it existed outside the realm of his control. Regardless of his motives, he'd done everything in his considerable power to squelch each juncture where Fae and Sidhe came together.

Her court, the Midnight Court, had been a centerpiece for combined magic. After Oberon ordered it disbanded, she and Titania had moved it...elsewhere. For a long while, she'd been certain Oberon would find out and put a stop to it, but he had a lazy streak a mile wide, and he'd never dug too deep. Nighttime festivals where everyone danced beneath twinkling stars flourished, until the land switched to perpetual daylight.

She'd been certain it was Oberon's backhanded way of punishing them, but Titania assured her that wasn't it at all. They'd taken care to erase revelers' memories of those enchanted gatherings, so a snitch in the crowd couldn't have been the problem. Hell, they'd even silenced the nightingales. She hugged her arms tighter around her legs and smiled as pleasant recollections of warm, lazy nights buffeted her. Rather like a cross between Beltane and Lughnasadh, there'd been plenty of laughter and sex and trading of all sorts.

Joy was a powerful motivator, a heady inspiration.

How long could she live on memories? The question curled her lip into a sneer. Apparently, forever. Faery's gates were no longer open to her, the Midnight Court long shuttered.

A breathy sigh rocked her, followed by another. Feeling sorry for herself wasn't her style. She'd get over this rough patch. Soon. Nothing had changed except she'd allowed herself to long for the impossible.

Everything that happened in this remote outpost occurred—or didn't—because of things she did. Exercising that level of control should have been satisfying, but it wasn't. Letting her daughter go—after endless arguments where she'd threatened to leave regardless—was one of the hardest things Auril had ever done. It meant she'd be alone forever, but what kind of life had she condemned Dariyah to? She squeezed her eyes shut tight. She'd done the best she could. Ensured the child lived and flourished, so the power within her could find its potential.

More drill sergeant than Mother, she'd trained the girl's magic. Taught her to harness her raw ability to protect herself. And she'd hidden her true name. Names have incalculable power. So long as Dariyah didn't know hers, no one could wrest if from her and use it against her. Auril's guts twisted into a physical ache. She'd followed her daughter, scrying her location and some of her activities over the eons they'd been separated. Each glimpse was a two-edged sword, mixing relief with a pervasive sorrow. She'd never lay eyes on her daughter again. She should have come to terms with that reality long since.

Should have.

Dariyah was alive. Knowing she'd survived should have been enough, but it wasn't. Many a night Auril tossed and turned. Sleep was elusive because she longed to wrap her arms around her daughter and feel the beat of her heart. Seeing her in visions, in imagery that ebbed and flowed, wasn't the same. Not even close.

Pushing upright from the spot she'd been crouched near her favorite scrying pool, she strode toward a cave. She visited it every afternoon at just this time. It was one of the patterns she'd maintained no matter what else was going on. Not that anything ever happened to disturb her routine. Sometimes, she wished something would, and then she offered up prayers to the goddess and said she hadn't meant it.

Monotony and boredom were preferable to unknown elements infiltrating her tiny corner of the universe.

Light flickered and flashed off the walls of a rounded cave studded with quartz formations. The lights came from the core of this world and bounced off the surface of a large, subterranean lake. Unlike Faery, this world wasn't inclined to talk. Strange, since she and it were the only sentient entities here. Auril had moved past lonely a few centuries ago, but the land endured. Silent, stoic, and ostensibly without needs of its own.

She'd visited the cave so often, she'd worn a path in the rocky dirt. Following it, she walked to the spot she always sat. Energy converged just there and made her future-seeing easier. Not that she had to conserve power. Nothing to use it for here, but she was cautious by nature. Just because no one had breached the borders of her lair didn't mean it couldn't happen.

At least she was past the worst of her spate of self-pity. She reminded herself nothing had altered except her focus. Looking backward wasn't productive. All it did was make her sad. She shook herself from head to toe before settling on her haunches on damp sand a handspan from the murky water. By all the gods and goddesses, she was still a queen, and she damned well needed to act like one. Her title had been conferred by Danu herself in a joint ceremony with Titania.

It had been very hush-hush, and Oberon hadn't been invited. The old geezer had been livid when he broke through Danu's barrier shielding the ritual from plain view. And even more outraged when the goddess sent him packing. The memory still brought a smile.

Auril twisted her mouth into a grimace. How Titania had continued to stand by her consort after all his shenanigans was tough to comprehend, but it was a sore topic. She and her sister never discussed him, for obvious reasons. If she'd been the one shackled to Oberon, she'd have cut off his dick and muffled his smart mouth with spells long ago.

The thought turned her grimace into a vicious grin. If she ever walked beneath Faery's skies again, the first thing she'd do would be to hang Oberon in effigy in the Midnight Court. Voodoo borrowed a page from her court, and she'd make the noose feel so authentic, the king of Faery would go running for his spell book in search of an antidote.

Sucking air to the very bottom of her lungs, she blew it out and then repeated the action a few times to center herself. A low hum began at the base of her spine and flowed upward, telling her the day's scrying session was well in hand. She preferred the outdoor pond she'd been settled next to, but power resided within the cave, and it fueled her efforts. With her arms extended in front of her and power arcing from her fingertips, she shut her earth eyes and switched to her psychic view.

The surface of the lake developed waves that swished back and forth before parting to form something that reminded her of a stage. At first it remained empty, its polished boards glistening gold in the odd light from the cave. Figures ebbed and flowed, not clear enough to make out beyond there being three of them. Auril waited. She'd been here before. The vision would speak to her in its own time.

Keep breathing, she instructed, certain of her magic, of her innate ability. Out of all her skills, her seer ability had never failed. The edges of the vision started curling in on themselves. Her eyes widened as shock rattled her equanimity. She sprang to her feet, hands still outstretched, and sent a jolt of enchantment dead center into the fading tableau.

"Reveal," she shouted. "I command you."

The vision should have shaped right up. It didn't, but at least it stopped collapsing. "That's right," Auril crooned. "Show me your truth."

Naught about today was panning out as she'd expected. Why should this be any different? She'd anticipated a gradual unfolding of a series of images for her to decrypt. The messages that came to her this way were never clear-cut.

Nothing slow and steady here, though. One minute, the perimeter circling the stage was about to implode, the next Titania, Dariyah, and a man who looked familiar burst into view. Heads together, the three of them were talking among themselves, their features carved into anxious expressions.

Titania flinched, and then straightened and turned. If she'd been in the cave, she'd have been staring dead into Auril's eyes. "Sister"—she tossed her head in a gesture so familiar, it smote Auril—"we shall be there soon."

The tableau burst from the inside outward in a blaze of reds and violets, leaving her staring at motes of light. Auril rubbed her eyes, not trusting anything. How had Titania sensed her across worlds and time? What was Dariyah doing with her sister?

What in the unholy fuck had happened since she'd last seen Dariyah in a vision? Her daughter had been in some kind of arcade playing cards with cat hairs clinging to her clothing and a human in thrall.

About the only answer that rose to the surface was the male Fae's identity. He was Cynwrigg ap Llyr, first in line for Faery's throne. Did his appearance with Titania mean Oberon was gone?

"A queen can dream," she muttered, breaking the silence stretching through the cavern. More truths marched across her mind. Dariyah must have told Titania where to find her. It was the only way her sister could have discovered this out-of-the-way realm.

Titania had said "we." Presumably, it meant all of them would arrive soon. The implication punched her in the guts. Her heart beat like a trip hammer; excitement raced through her. Dariyah would actually be here next to her, in her arms where she could pat her, touch her. Stroke hair out of her face and make all the maternal noises she'd avoided for fear of spoiling the child.

She's not a child anymore. Her implacable inner voice

brought her up short. *Better to love and accept the woman she's grown into.*

Her mouth bent into a wry grin. Grand advice. Who knew how it would play out? Dariyah's magic existed in a class of its own. What had she done with her talents? Had the time come for her to stroll into Faery and take her rightful place amongst its leaders? Auril hadn't disclosed that part of her future-seeing to her daughter. She'd told her to steer clear of Faery because her mixed blood could spell her death—until she came into her own and was strong enough to claim her birthright.

Auril sank into a crouch, kneeling next to the dark waters of the lake. Its surface had quieted, but not for long. Once again, she extended her hands and bounced jolts of lightning off the water's surface. "Show me the future," she intoned. "Do it now. No more games."

Enchantment sheeted from her, marrying her mind to the universe. If her viewing of Titania had been true —and it almost had to be—worlds had shifted on their axes. She'd shed one skin when she left Faery. Maybe it was time to shed the one she'd worn ever since.

Breath burst from her, and she didn't make the slightest effort to mute her triumph. A celebration might be premature, but she was done pussyfooting around and playing nice with destiny. If the Queen of Air and Darkness was about to rise from her self-imposed crypt, she was more than ready to make it happen with her daughter and sister by her side.

The three of them should be unbreakable. She'd seen it often enough in dreams and visions. "Not should be, will be. No more shoulds for me." She breathed the words and turned her attention to her nascent spell shaping the lake's dark water to her purposes.

CHAPTER ONE, CYN

"What was that?" I focused intently on Titania and dropped a truth net over her. It wasn't respectful, but difficult times called for unusual solutions. I'd felt her telepathic magic and wanted to make damn good and sure she wasn't engaging in a covert conversation with Oberon.

She skewered me with a baleful glance out of her unnerving golden eyes. "Since when do you have the right to question me, Cynwrigg ap Llyr?"

I held her gaze. "Would you expect less of me, my lady? With everything that's befallen us, caution has to work in our favor."

"Aye, lad, but last I checked we were on the same side." She made a sour face. "The one standing against darkness." She'd been separating her long white hair into sections and proceeded to weave them into plaits.

Angling my head to one side, I regarded her. Was she being purposely obtuse?

Meanwhile, Dariyah balanced a spell between upraised hands. "Are we leaving, or not?"

Titania furled a white brow and spun one hand in a circle. I got it. She was ordering me to release my truth casting so we could get on with things. Backing down isn't my style. Dariyah didn't require my intervention to keep her safe, but savage possessiveness shot through me. I'd do everything I could to ensure we didn't put Dariyah, or her mother, at risk.

I remembered Auril well enough. A formidable figure, she'd had to wend her way through Oberon's various prohibitions, which had grown stricter with the passing years. Now that I knew who Dariyah's mother was, I was ashamed I hadn't figured it out on my own. The family resemblance was obvious. Auril had the same lush, red locks, Valkyrie build, and striking features. The only difference was their eyes. Where Dariyah's were a clear green, Auril's were silver.

"You have to trust someone." Titania's voice was soft, and her masses of hair had been coaxed into a dozen plaits hanging down her back to knee level.

"Answer my question"—my tone was gruff—"and we can be on our way."

"So you don't trust me." Titania sounded wounded, but part of it was interlaced magic, designed to make me feel guilty for doubting her.

"Trust has nothing to do with it," I retorted. "At this moment, I don't trust anyone." I could have stopped there, but I plowed on. "Remember Aedan?"

"Aye. The two of you were inseparable as children."

"He joined forces with your consort and became a traitor to Faery."

Titania steepled her fingers together. "Poor Faery. The rot has spread. No wonder she's struggling."

"Answer me," I urged. "So we can be gone before Oberon shows up with reinforcements." I meant it as a reminder. No matter where we went, we had to be gone quickly.

The queen of Faery narrowed her eyes. "You win this round...kinsman. I sensed Auril scrying and reached through her spell. We share enough blood to make such feats possible."

Her words trilled off my truth net, clean and pure. I disabled the weave, directing it to become one with the ether. "Thank you, my lady."

After a muttered, "Jesus, I hate wasting magic," Dariyah kicked a portal open and dragged us through after her.

"What you'd hate more would be bringing trouble down on your mother's head," I told her.

"I resent that," Titania said stiffly.

Turning, I got a good, hard look at her. When we'd first breached the walls of her prison, she'd looked like a ghost, wraith-thin and clinging to life by the barest of margins. Her color was better, and an approximation of the queen I remembered stood tall in her richly embroidered silken robes.

"Did you talk with Mother, or just see her?" Dariyah asked.

"Both. I told her we would be there soon."

"Was she angry?" Dariyah quirked one brow into a question mark.

"I don't believe so, child." Titania frowned. "My sister never could leave off dredging through the past or seeking clues about the future. Her energy was obvious today, and so I latched onto it."

"Are you wondering why you hadn't felt it before?" I asked a logical question.

"Eh, Mother probably couldn't penetrate the shrouding around the miniature castle Titania was living in," Dariyah muttered. "Or maybe the runes on the door had something to do with it."

"How'd you remove them?" Titania asked.

"One glyph at a time." Dariyah offered a facsimile of a smile.

"I wondered how that would go." The queen closed her teeth over her lower lip.

"How what would go?" I asked in a sharper tone than I'd meant to employ. Shit. I was edgy as fuck, and I needed to tone it down. Leaving Titania's erstwhile jail should have settled me somewhat, except it hadn't. Trying for stealth, I checked the integrity of Dariyah's spell to make certain she'd blocked our tracks.

"Satisfied?" Dariyah elbowed me.

"Um, yeah. Better safe than sorry."

Twisting, she regarded me with an unreadable expression. "Not my first rodeo running from bad guys. How do you suppose I managed before you came along?"

"Good for you, dear," Titania chimed in.

I winced. "Ouch. I guess I deserved that. From both of you."

Dariyah gripped my wrist. "No one is more interested in keeping Mother safe than me. No one. If I didn't care, I'd have beat a path to her door. Always being alone is harder than I ever imagined."

"You never exactly embrace it," Titania agreed. "On good days, my solitude was tolerable, but there weren't very many of them. Auril's situation was different than mine, though. She chose her destiny; mine was foisted onto me."

"She chose my destiny too," Dariyah said softly.

"You wouldn't have cared for the alternative," the queen countered.

"I can think of at least one or two beyond Mother aborting me." Dariyah set her mouth in a tight line.

Their argument circled me back to Titania's latest unanswered question. Not that Faery's queen owed me jack, but sidestepping my queries was getting old. "What did you mean about wondering how 'that' would go?" I glanced Titania's way.

A cool stare was all the response I got before she murmured, "The child's magic is different enough to unlock secrets. In this instance, it untangled the power of those runes holding me in place."

Meanwhile the edges of Dariyah's teleport spell had developed pearlescent edges. I knew her well enough to read tension in the set of her shoulders and closed-off expression. She'd asked if Auril was angry. They'd been the first words out of her mouth. It might mean her mother wouldn't even be here.

"Almost there." Dariyah breathed the words in Gaelic.

"Have you not been back since you went out on your own?" Titania asked.

"Mother made me promise to stay away. For both our sakes."

Titania nodded. It could have been approval or something else entirely. "My sister is made of steel. I tried to channel her resolve after Oberon swept me neatly out of the way."

"Why'd he do that?" I asked, not expecting an answer. When she began talking, it surprised me.

"I became…inconvenient," she replied. "His fixation on Faery being only for Fae grated on me. I'd always treated fairly with all of Faery's citizenry. The mix of magics nurtured the land and made us stronger. My consort didn't view things through the same lens. We quarreled more and more frequently, and I took to living elsewhere. I hadn't spoken with him in perhaps a couple of years when a phalanx of his men shanghaied me. I fought, but I was no match for twenty-five trained warriors. I'd no sooner dispatched one than two more jumped in my path."

"Why didn't you teleport away from the fight?" I asked.

"Running isn't my style." Her upper lip curled into a sneer. "Those were my subjects too. I'd be damned if I'd let them have the upper hand."

Dariyah let go of my arm and patted the queen's shoulder. I expected a harsh rebuke, but Titania didn't say a word. Perhaps she'd rethought the prohibition against touching her in the time she'd been away. Even if she hadn't, she'd had a long while to recognize her error in not exiting while she had a chance.

Her gaze sharpened and zeroed in on me. "If I'd known what Oberon had in store for me, I wouldn't have tripped over my own pride," she growled. "Once his henchmen dropped me in the place you found me, it took months before I understood I was stuck there for good. That no one was coming to free me."

"You must have tried to escape," I prodded, mining for details.

"Nay. I wilted and gave up immediately." Her tone dripped sarcasm. She took a swing at me but was too far away to connect. "Of course, I attempted to flee. I couldn't drill through the runes on the door. Not even a glyph at a time."

"Stop sparring with each other." Dariyah broke into what was indeed turning into an argument.

Her spell frittered to nothing, and a sun-dappled world shaped up around us. Auril must have been waiting because she raced through a break in a dense thicket and threw her arms around Dariyah. Titania joined them, threading her arms around her sister and niece.

The similarities between Auril and Dariyah were even more pronounced now that I saw them next to each other. Same slant to their cheekbones. Same strong, square chin. Same high forehead. Auril wore garments that appeared to have been woven from a combination of wool and plant fibers. Did sheep graze on this world? Or had some other animal donated clothing material?

I felt like an anachronism, an unneeded fifth wheel, but neither could I turn away. Tears streamed down the women's cheeks. Some turned to bits of gold and gems when they hit the ground. Why had Dariyah assumed Auril would be angry? From what I could gather, the Queen of Air and Darkness was as thrilled to be reunited as her daughter was.

Feeling like a voyeur, but not wanting to intrude, I finally walked to a nearby flat stone and sat on it, taking in a world I'd never known existed. Ysir had said only two of the outer worlds supported life. This was clearly one of the outer realms, but the air was thick and smelled sweet. Since we'd already visited two of these places, this made one more, which suggested Ysir had underestimated their numbers when he took it upon himself to map the universe.

How had Auril located it? Desperation combined with trial-and-error, no doubt. She'd been driven by a powerful motivator: finding a spot where she could stop running long enough to raise her daughter. Except she'd remained here long after Dariyah left. Why had she been afraid to return? Clearly, Titania knew about her pregnancy, but none of the rest of us did. Rumors had flown thick and fast for a while, until the next juicy bit of gossip hit, and then Auril was forgotten. She probably had no idea she could have slipped back into Faery and taken up the mantle of the Midnight Court once again.

The hidden court no one talked about, but we all knew existed.

As I thought about Ysir, I recalled his description of the outer worlds as desolate places. This was anything but. Rolling meadows dotted with flowers, flowering shrubbery, and bisected by a rushing creek with many branches stretched as far as I could see. Unlike many worlds, the sky was blue with a single sun suspended midheaven. A red fox walked up to me and nuzzled my hand. Songbirds trilled from trees, and hawks swooped and dove through the air.

The women's tears had dried; they were chattering a mile a minute in Gaelic. I could have listened in, but it seemed more honest to join the conversation. After getting my feet under me, I walked toward them. The tears that had turned to gems glittered in stray rays from the sun. I hadn't paid them much heed when they'd fallen, but they caught my attention now. Fae didn't cry gems. The only creatures I knew of whose tears turned into a king's ransom were unicorns and dragons.

Had Dariyah's father been one or the other?

The women hadn't acknowledged my presence. I cleared my throat; three sets of eyes turned toward me. I tipped an imaginary top hat and said, "Auril. It's been a while."

Peals of laughter rolled from her throat. In a voice a bit higher than Dariyah's, she said, "You always were a master of understatement, Cynwrigg."

Dariyah looked from her mother to me and back again. "Of course, you'd know one another."

"Aye, child," Auril replied. "All with Fae blood are linked. Including you."

Somewhere between Titania's prison and here, Dariyah had dropped her Witch glamour. She twirled, gathering it into place. "Ah, but I quit being Fae to avoid discovery. Meet Dari, the Witch."

Auril cocked her head to one side. Jets of power probed her daughter's disguise. "Not bad," she said at last.

"It fooled Oberon." Dariyah sounded mildly defensive.

"Pfft. Not all that hard to accomplish," Titania muttered.

"He always was lazy," Auril agreed cheerfully. "Maybe someday you'll tell me why you stuck with him."

"I've had a whole lot of years to contemplate just that topic, but he's not worth the breath to talk about," Titania said firmly. "Are you ready to come home, Sister?"

Auril's smile faded. "I'm not sure. Share a meal with me, and we'll talk. I've seen...things. Wisps and bits in the water and in my glass too. It might be time for many elements to come together."

"Some things don't change," Dariyah noted sourly. "You still talk in riddles."

Auril dropped an arm around her shoulders. "Riddles kept first me, and then us, safe. Don't be so quick to discount them. People look where they expect to find things."

"And when they don't?" I asked.

"Well then, they focus on something else, and whatever secret I was harboring remained secure." Auril raked me from head to toe with her gaze. "My daughter tells me you've befriended her, taken her past Faery's gates. Thank you for doing what I could not."

"You didn't have to stay gone." I kicked my shoulders back and met her silvery gaze.

"Aye. I did. 'Twasn't my time, and if I'd been closer, 'twould have been that much harder to maintain distance betwixt Dari and me."

"I can't believe how alike the two of you are." Titania shook her head. "It's like looking at twins."

"Another reason to keep Dariyah and me out of Faery at the same time," Auril murmured.

"No one saw through my glamour, although I admit it only altered my magical signature not my appearance," Dariyah protested and rolled her eyes. "Damn it, Mother, I'm not ten anymore. I've done okay working things out for myself."

Auril looked askance at her daughter. "Maybe. Whatever possessed you to work for Oberon? Surely, you knew who he was."

"Of course I did," Dariyah snapped. "I needed work, and—"

"Bullcrap!" Auril spat back. "You fell into thrall, hooked by Faery's allure. The land's call is like a Siren song for Fae. Even those masquerading as something else."

"If I had it to do over," Dariyah huffed, "I'd do the same thing."

"Of course you would, niece," Titania broke in. "For the same reason my sister just elucidated. Faery gets her claws into us all."

"We can stand here and argue"—Auril smiled softly—"or we could eat something. Frankly, I mowed through a whole lot of magic this afternoon, and I could do with a meal."

Titania's features sharpened into speculation. "You finally saw something with your infernal scrying, didn't you?"

Auril shrugged. "Perhaps. Sit and eat with me."

"Thank you for your offer of a meal." I kept my tone formal. "It's appreciated, and then I must guide Titania back to Faery. The land longs for her lost regent. All Oberon does of late is torment her."

Titania burst out laughing so raucously my cheeks grew warm. "I fail to see the humor in my words," I said stiffly.

When she was done hooting and cackling, she wiped

her streaming eyes. A surreptitious examination of the ground affirmed she wasn't the one shedding diamonds, rubies, and gold. "As if I require a guide to find my own land. Thank you for the offer, though."

"I shall see you safely back to Faery," I insisted. "If something happened to you betwixt here and there, I would never forgive myself."

Dariyah hooked an arm in with mine. "Let him play Sir Galahad," she told her aunt and mother. "He won't back off. I recognize the look on his face."

"The two of you are close enough you're familiar with his moods? I thought he was merely an associate." Auril's inspection of me took on a whole new layer of interest.

Before she spit out something to the effect I wasn't exactly son-in-law material, I said, "We are friends and associates. She needed help, but so did I. We fought Oberon's henchmen together, and she healed a rift beneath Faery."

I'd tried for diplomatic, but Dariyah took a direct approach. "Back off, Mother. Who I know well enough to read their expressions is none of your affair." She hip-butted me. "Come on. I know the way to my erstwhile home. Mom and Auntie can keep on catching up."

I didn't wait for her to ask again. The two crones made a formidable pair. Titania had been right about not requiring me—or my magic—to return to Faery, but I'd escort her nonetheless. It was the right thing to do, and she was still my queen.

"Who'd have thought I was related to Titania," Dariyah mused as we strode along quite a way ahead of Auril and her sister.

So long she was ruminating about family, I dove in. "Is this the first time you've shed tears that turned to gems?"

Dariyah's head flashed around. "What in the hell are you talking about?"

"Back there"—I jerked my chin in the direction we'd come from—"where the three of you were hugging and crying, gold and gems are all over the ground."

"Pfft. Don't be ridiculous."

"Why would I make something like that up?" I slid my hand around and captured the one she'd grasped my arm with.

"I don't know, but it's absurd."

"Is it? Want to go back and look?"

She shook her head. "No. Not really. I guess you'd have no reason to lie about something I could verify. Maybe Mother's magic has changed. Or they came from Titania."

"Titania was laughing her head off after I offered to accompany her to Faery. Her tears were just tears."

Dariyah's pace slowed. Twisting her head, she looked up at me. "What are you suggesting?"

"I believe they're yours, and it narrows the field for who your father might be."

A shudder ran through her. "Dragons and unicorns," she mumbled, sounding shaken. "Probably the former."

"Why?"

"When I was young, I had wing buds, but they fell off before I hit twenty. I assumed they were from my Sidhe blood."

"It's there too. At least I think it is." I tried for reassuring, but Dariyah wasn't buying it. The harder I worked to tease out who her father had been, the murkier things grew, but I'd be damned if I'd tell her as much.

"So Father was a Sidhe, but with a dragon somewhere in his family tree? That should restrict the possibilities considerably."

It did, but I built a ward around my mind and kept my mouth shut. As far as I knew, only one man met that description, and he hadn't been welcomed into polite company—or any company at all—for all the years of my memory.

"How much farther to your mother's house?" I asked.

"You're changing the subject." She stopped and spun to face me. "You know something, don't you?"

"It's your mother's right to disclose your parentage. Besides, I'm not certain of anything. How much farther?"

Her forehead furrowed into annoyed lines, probably because I hadn't been forthcoming, and she knew as much. "We're here." She barked a power word; an illusory curtain I'd totally missed went up in a puff of smoke.

A hut built of stones and mortar rose before us, surrounded by a riot of brilliant flowers and a white-painted porch. Dariyah stormed inside without a backward glance. I started to follow, but decided to wait for Titania and Auril. The least I could do was warn them I'd peeled the lid partway off Dariyah's personal Pandora's box.

CHAPTER TWO, DARIYAH

"Fuck." I drove a fist into a familiar wall, feeling the sting as my knuckles connected with it. Droplets of blood hung in the air before forming a glowing circle and arrowing back into my body. I'd forgotten that part. Nothing offering clues to our presence here was allowed to escape. Mother had spelled the house and everything around it, although as I'd grown older and less likely to skin my knees on things, she'd tightened the circle until it only included the house.

Interesting it was still in place. She hadn't appeared particularly concerned about our tears wetting the ground. Had I really shed gemstones? Or gold? I didn't believe it. Not that I'm much of a crier. I'm not. But I'd have noticed the glitter of gems scattered about.

Too twitchy to sit, I paced through the cottage where I'd grown up. A simple structure, it had a main room where we'd cooked, eaten, and read the scrolls Mother brought with us. A sleeping area was separated by a curtain, with a secondary sleeping space in a loft that spanned half the cottage. Mother had been forever adding onto the structure. A room with a tub sunken into the ground and lined with river rocks had been the most recent addition. Once it was done, she'd instructed water from a nearby hot spring to flow underground through a system of pipes and into the tub.

Before that, we'd bathed in the spring. I'd actually preferred it to what she jokingly referred to as indoor plumbing.

Mother...

My anger, always quick to ignite, was fading quickly. I owed her everything. She'd hidden my father's identity for a reason, probably more than one. Breath hissed through my teeth, and I unclenched my jaw. I'd taken my irritation out on Cyn. None of this was his fault. I'd been alone for so long, I'd forgotten how to get along with other people.

Mouth twisting into a wry grin, I thought about Midnight, my current companion. A large, black tomcat, he wasn't overly picky about my moods so long as I kept kibble in his dish.

Despite my irritation, it was wonderful to be back

here. The house held its own magic, and it smelled like Mother with her lupine, lemon, and brandy scents. I inhaled deeply; her distinctive fragrance washed through me like a balm. I'd lived here for the better part of forty years. It was the only home I'd ever known until I went out on my own, and even then I'd never settled anywhere for long.

Always on the run, afraid someone would ferret out what I was, I'd lived on the fringes of everything forever. It didn't make me good friend material for anyone beyond my cat. He didn't require much, and because he couldn't talk he didn't misunderstand me.

Pfft. I'd moved from being pissed to feeling sorry for myself. I needed to pull my head out of my ass before Mother and Titania got here, and I owed Cyn an apology. That part was imminently doable. It wouldn't get any easier for waiting, so I redirected my steps from the circle I'd been scribing around the perimeter of the living area and trotted back out the door.

Cynwrigg stood with his back to the house, leaning against a tree. Because I had a moment or two before he sensed my presence, I studied his tall, lean form. He employed a glamour too, but only for his Earth-self managing a busy casino in Reno, Nevada. His height was the same, but his glamour added a burly aspect to his graceful body. He'd dropped it when we fought Titania's guards. No need to siphon magic for anything other than our objective, which was freeing Faery's queen from her long captivity.

Garbed in dark trousers, a cream colored shirt with flowing sleeves, and scuffed leather boots, he cut an arresting figure. He could have been wearing sackcloth and his natural grace would have shown through. Long, pale hair framed his strong-boned face, falling to the middle of his back. When the light caught it exactly right, it shimmered with coppery highlights. I couldn't see his eyes from my vantage point, but they were a fascinating combination of gold and silver with copper centers. Naturally, his glamour hid them while he was on Earth. No human had eyes like that.

He turned slowly and walked toward me, forehead furrowed with concern and the tips of his ears poking through his fall of hair. "Better?"

I shrugged. "Yeah. Apologies for taking out my frustration on you."

"I understand." He reached me and placed a hand on each of my shoulders. "It's a lot to take in. You've discovered things you didn't know about Auril. It's natural for you to be annoyed she wasn't more forthcoming. There's something about the magic in this place. Do you feel... odd?"

I'd been too wrapped up in my own machinations to notice much of anything. Damn it. One more glitch on my part. I knew better than to go blithely forward without checking my surroundings for possible potholes. Things I could fall into if I weren't careful.

Leading with my heart instead of my brain had almost been my downfall more than once. I felt safe here, but it was a weak suck of an excuse. Where were Mother and Titania? They should have caught up with us by now.

"Dariyah?" Heat from Cyn's hands seared my shoulders and traveled through me. His touch ignited something primitive, and it took all my self-control not to lean into him, wrap my arms around his broad back, and lose myself in his whiskey-and-wildflower scent. Piquant, heady, it made me long for a life in Faery.

With him.

Eh. Before I totally lost it and turned into a simpering, needy female, I mumbled, "I'm all right. Haven't noticed anything unusual, but then I didn't look, either. Hang on."

Stretching my power around me, I ducked from beneath his touch, jabbing and probing. I've always been strong, but power jumped to my command, surprising me with its intensity. I narrowed my eyes. "Something's different."

"You are, child." Mother's voice preceded her figure as she and Titania strolled toward us, arm in arm.

I waited until they reached the spot I stood, and said, "You have to say more than that."

A corner of Mother's mouth twisted downward. "I don't have to, but in this instance I will. I set protections around you before you left me. Safeguards to keep your identity hidden. Those protections do not work here, so the moment you crossed the border into these lands, my spell dissipated, and your magic was free to flow at its full strength."

"It's why your tears turned to gold and gems," Titania tossed out.

The anger that had consumed me earlier flared up like a bonfire, roaring through my body. "You constrained my magic?" My voice was shrill, but I didn't seem to have control over much of anything.

Mother angled her head to one side, regarding me with a gesture so familiar it arrowed right into my heart. "Not so much constrained as altered some elements about your skills." She rolled her shoulders back. "If you'd traipsed out of here like gangbusters, power shooting from you at all angles, you'd have captured someone's attention. It would only have been a matter of time—and not very much of it—before word of your existence filtered to Faery.

"What I did bought you time to modulate your talents, to employ them in ways that didn't paint a target on your back." She paused to take a measured breath and blow it out. "One reality I couldn't alter is your mixed blood. And unless something has changed in Faery, it still carries a death sentence."

"Working on that," Cyn spoke up. "We have to rewrite the covenant, but I'm waiting until we have a full contingent of delegates on the court."

"What happened to them?" Titania furled her white brows Cyn's way.

"All the Fae on the court but one were spies for Oberon, traitors to Faery. The unicorn who sits on the court killed them, and I fed the remains to the land," Cyn replied.

Titania rubbed her veined hands together. "Oooh. Good show, Cynwrigg. Wish I'd been there to see it."

"You'll be party to plenty of bloodshed," Cyn reassured her. "We are far from done."

"Your mentioned Cousin Aedan, before." Titania slitted her eyes. "Was he one of them?"

"He was." Cyn's reply lacked inflection, but I'd seen the pain in his eyes when we'd consigned his cousin to certain death at Faery's hands. He'd done what needed doing, no matter what it cost, and I respected the hell out of him for it.

"I figured as much. He always played the lackey to Oberon. Made excuses for every horrid spate of words or deeds." The queen flattened her mouth into a grim expression. "Oberon promised him Faery's throne."

Cyn's features darkened as the full weight of her statement sank in. "But I was in the way, eh?"

"They were working on that when Oberon ousted me." Breath hissed through Titania's teeth. "I always assumed my protests against such a move were the final straw behind my exile. We may not have been talking, but we kept eyes on each other from afar."

"Join me. Please." Mother started along the flagstone walkway toward the front door I'd left open.

My image of Faery was shifting by the moment. I'd always envisioned the home that was barred to me as an idyllic spot full of merry mages living in verdant forests. Never in my wildest imaginings would I have guessed it was a sinister place filled with court intrigue and jockeying for position. That sort of thing had fallen out of vogue with the close of the nineteenth century.

Titania strolled after her sister. Cyn placed a hand under my elbow. "Mostly, Faery is similar to your imaginings. Those involved in plotting and scheming are few and far between."

Laying aside him helping himself to my thoughts, I twisted to glance at him. "Not so sure about that. I culled a pretty damned long list of conspirators out of Aedan's head."

He drew his fair brows together. "I've been thinking about that. Oberon couldn't have known Aedan would be captured, but he's shrewd enough to have recognized my cousin as a weak link in the chain. If he really promised Aedan the throne, it was a manipulation to gain his cooperation."

"What are you saying?" I cut in. "That some of the names on that interminable list are innocent?"

"I suspect so," Cynwrigg replied, "but it makes our task much more difficult."

"Because we have to truth net everyone." I leaned against him. The specter of testing that many individuals was overwhelming, unless— "We could do it in groups," I speculated out loud.

"There are many ways we can accomplish sorting friend from traitor. My bent would be to task the unicorns and maybe the newly seated council members —once they're elected."

I nodded. He was used to delegating, where I'd always worked alone. Not having to do everything myself was a refreshing change.

"Dari. Cynwrigg. Come eat." Mother's voice floated out the door.

"That was fast." Cyn started along the path.

I laughed. "Mother hates to cook, so she uses magic liberally. I don't think we ever had the same dish twice."

"How about you?"

"One of the best parts of modern life is takeout," I replied as we crossed beneath the lintel. The same lush scents that had soothed my earlier anger surrounded us.

This time food smells mingled with Mother's lupine-lemon-brandy essence.

Mother and Titania were seated at either end of a table just big enough to accommodate four. Two steaming tureens sat on trivets. I stopped by the sink and pumped water to rinse my hands and face. Cyn stood next to me, waiting for me to be done.

"What happened to your hair, child?" Mother asked while I was drying my hands on a towel, leaving blood and black streaks.

"Titania's guards happened to it." I made a snorting noise. "It'll grow back, but the guards won't. We killed all of them. Those who weren't quite dead when we left probably are by now."

Titania set down her fork. "I already knew as much, but it's simply splendid to hear it out loud. They understood full well the extent of their transgressions holding me against my will. I'm glad they're dead."

Mother shot an intense look at her sister. "Did they... harm you?"

"They knew better. Even in my depleted condition, if they'd touched me I could have emptied their power and used it to replenish my own."

I sat in what had been my customary spot to Mother's right and helped myself to dinner. My stomach had begun growling while I stood at the sink, reminding me I'd long since blown through the calories I'd consumed at the casino. Cyn joined us, taking the one remaining chair and spooning food into his bowl.

"Thank you for preparing supper for us." He bowed his head in Mother's direction.

"Thank you for eating with me. Since Dariyah left, my only companions have been the birds and animals."

"Betimes, they're far more trustworthy than people," Titania said sourly and filled her bowl again.

For the next few minutes, the only sounds in the cottage were the clink of carved wooden tableware against wooden bowls. Mother had crafted everything we'd need once we arrived here. It had taken a bit of trial and error to find items that held up to everyday use without a constant infusion of magic.

Mother glanced up from her meal. "We must discuss the immediate future," she said.

I stared into her eyes. "Before we launch into that, how about a couple of my agenda items?"

"Such as?" She arched both red brows.

"My name, for starters."

Mother shook her head. "My reasons for hiding it have not gone away. Names have power, child, and—"

Maybe it was her calling me *child*, but something inside of me cracked into a whole lot of pieces and scraped against one another. "Everyone at this table is privy to their true name except me," I gritted. "While you maybe had a right to withhold it when I was young, that excuse has run its course." I snapped my fingers. "Come on. Pony up."

Mother's features took on a mulish look I remembered all too well. She pushed to her feet and spread her arms wide. "We—the four of us—are essential to Faery's future. We must use our time wisely and plan our next steps. I will uncover your true name eventually, but that moment has not yet arrived." Breath swooshed from her before she went on. "I assume your next 'agenda item' relates to your father. My response is the same. I will reveal his identity when the time is right. It's not."

Splaying the flats of my hands on the table, I rocketed to my feet, staring her down. "Then we have nothing to talk about, and I'm leaving."

"Sit down, now." Titania didn't raise her voice. She didn't have to. It resonated with command.

My gaze skittered in her direction. "I don't report to you."

"The hell you don't. Sit down."

Something about the way she said it told me I'd reached a choice point. Either I thumbed my nose at all of them and left, or I laid my personal needs aside for now. If I chose door number one, I'd return to my solitary existence—with my cat. No more Faery. Probably no more Cynwrigg—because I'd be too ashamed to face him.

That's the thing about insights. They slap you where it hurts. I may have been alone forever, but I wasn't totally thoughtless. And I'd never viewed myself as selfish at all. Quite the contrary. Heh. My mirror was obviously distorted. In the absence of feedback from anyone except my cat—and the kitties who'd come before him—I'd developed an unrealistic opinion of myself.

I felt Cyn's eyes on me. My face heated, and my butt connected to the chair I'd just vacated, but I didn't look at him.

"You sit too. This isn't about you." Titania aimed her words at Mother. At least I wasn't the only bad actor in the room.

Mother tossed her head and sank back into her chair. Her mouth curled into a wry expression. "Right you are, Sister."

Hot words scoured the back of my throat. I held them in place. No one wanted to hear me whine about being treated unfairly. Only children did that. "What's next?" I tried for a bright smile but didn't manage much more than a grimace.

"We must resurrect the Midnight Court," Mother said. "Immediately."

"Will its combined magics be sufficient to defeat Oberon?" Titania leaned forward, her golden eyes glowing with anticipation.

"I believe so." Auril nodded. "It's what I've seen in my future-seeking."

"But the Midnight Court was in full swing when Oberon was still running things. Didn't appear to slow him down at all," Cynwrigg spoke up.

"He has lost much of his power," Titania said, "and—"

"Ha!" I broke in. "Suspected as much. I flaunted my Witch glamour all around him, and he never saw through it."

"Probably because he wasn't looking," Titania commented dryly.

"Nope," I replied emphatically. "Once he fired me—and didn't pay me and sent spies to fuck with me—we turned into enemies. Surely then, he'd have probed for information he could have used to destroy me."

"Maybe. He can be dense as a rock, but it's a mistake to underestimate him," Titania said. "He retains the bond with Faery, and her magic is enormous."

Mother flapped a hand at her sister. "It's why we have to bring the Midnight Court back. It's a way to strengthen Faery so she can sever the bond."

"Have you actually seen that event? Oberon's link with the land breaking?" Titania's tone was sharp, penetrating.

"Not exactly," Mother said. "But I've seen enough to

make me believe it's possible. We can add our combined magics to her efforts, and—"

Cynwrigg cleared his throat. "The land should be bonded with me. She borrowed Dariyah's body to talk with us."

"Really?" Interest flared from Mother.

"Aye. Tell us all about it. Spare no details." Titania spun one hand in a get-on-with-it motion.

"Be quick," Mother instructed.

I grinned, and she said, "What?"

"I'd forgotten how high-handed you can be. Guess I come by my bossy streak honestly. Faery was gentle with me, but I'd healed the rift in her foundations. That was another time she could have strip mined my magic and left me nothing but a husk. She didn't, and—"

"Dariyah. Focus." Mother's voice chopped through the wonder Faery's presence engendered. Gathering my thoughts into a more cohesive whole, I started again.

CHAPTER THREE, CYN

Because no one was paying me much heed, I managed a bit of surface mind skimming while Dariyah relayed her time playing host to Faery. At Titania's prodding, she sketched out how Faery had wrested magic away from her to heal the rift. Not surprisingly, Auril knew a lot more than she was letting on. Dariyah's birth was actually an elemental part of an overarching plan hatched long ago. Important enough to force Auril's exit from Faery, the scheme was finally coming full circle.

I hadn't been able to glean anything close to the complete plan, other than it would change the course of magic for the rest of eternity. Titania was privy to much, but not all of it. Her mind was far more difficult to access. Since I was doing my damnedest to be invisible, I didn't dare risk poking harder.

Probably the only reason I gleaned anything from Auril was because a thin stream of power flowed continuously, maintaining wards and suchlike. The ever-present outflow offered a natural indentation where I could hide in hollow places and remain undetected. Even that wouldn't have protected my incursion for long, though, if Auril's attention hadn't been fixed firmly on her daughter.

Despite their squabble over Dariyah's name and her parentage, I didn't believe she would have up and left. She'd have been walking out on far more than her long-lost mother, and she knew as much.

But this wasn't my affair. Or my battle, so I'd remained quiet. I'd been proud of her for knowing when to back down, for understanding this was so much bigger than a power struggle between her and her mother. Auril had never spent much visible time in Faery. She'd been there, but it took effort to find her. As a Fae who preferred the company of Sidhe, her retreat had been the Midnight Court.

Oberon considered it a slap in the face. Many a time, he'd complained we had a court and did not need another one. He also resented the hell out of the clandestine ceremony when Danu had crowned Auril the Queen of Air and Darkness. After a spectacular blowout where Oberon had done a fine old job splitting Faery into those for him and those against him, Auril moved the Midnight Court far away.

She believed in her reign, but she respected Faery too much to turn it into a battleground for competing ideologies.

Auril shook her head as if something had lodged in her hair. I executed a quiet retreat. I'd discovered all I could with stealth. From here on in, it was up to how much of a team we actually were. Whether they'd truly include me or not remained to be seen.

"That's about it," Dariyah was saying.

"You've done well, Daughter." Auril smiled.

Dariyah blew out a long breath. "I didn't do any of it for your approval."

Auril's grin widened. "Makes it even better. We should return to Faery to the former lair where my court came together. Then we'll get the word out and see who remembers the good times."

"Everyone," Titania said succinctly. "They'll come back. Rumors of your imminent return circulated for hundreds of years after you left."

"Do you think we should make inroads into Oberon's contingent of spies and traitors, first?" I asked, concerned Auril and Titania's appearance could catapult his timeline into hyperdrive. And cause Faery untold grief.

Titania's escape might have already done that. I'd find out quick enough once we returned.

Auril got to her feet and said, "Follow me. I want to draw you a timeline of what I've seen." On her way out the door, she picked up a pointed stick leaning in a corner. Made sense she'd have a drawing implement since paper wasn't available here. A few scrolls sat on a shelf affair on one wall, but presumably those were lore books she'd brought with her. Most mages would rather cut off a hand than deface vellum with our history inscribed on its leaves.

We ended up standing in a semi-circle around Auril. The day was pleasant, warm and breezy. Did it ever get cold here? Or dark?

With a few explanations as she went, Auril drafted a series of overlapping events in the smooth dirt on one side of the flagstone path. "This represents an amalgamation of many, many scrying sessions," she cautioned as she straightened, set the stick aside, and folded her arms under her breasts. "But there's been enough continuity to my visions, I believe this"—she pointed at the timeline—"is fairly accurate."

"How long have you known Faery was in trouble?" Titania fixed her golden eyes on her sister.

"I only figured it out a couple of weeks ago. My scrying developed an urgency that hadn't been there before, and I kept seeing blood spattered all over the ground, dragons bugling their fears, and a herd of upset unicorns. I'd been considering breaking my exile and returning, and then I saw the three of you."

"And assumed destiny would find you, even all the way out here." Titania made a wry face.

"What I assumed," Auril retorted, "was my future-seeing was imminent. No longer pegged to a distant point that hadn't happened yet, prophecies were rising to meet me."

I'm a planner. It's both blessing and curse. Not that I always have the luxury of planning. Mostly, when things turn to shit, I end up forced into a split-second decision, like had happened with my cousin, Aedan, when I secured him behind a magical barrier.

"Before we go," I said, "let's get a few more loose ends tacked down."

"Such as?" Auril's tone suggested one more cook in the kitchen wasn't welcome.

"Who will do what, and when?" I replied. "For example, I will reconvene the court and assess if we have enough candidates for the empty seats to hold an immediate election. We're not waiting until the next festival. Not this time. I want to rewrite the covenant as soon as the new delegates are seated."

"What about the traitors?" Dariyah asked.

"Needs to be a parallel track," I told her. "Ferret out

the low-hanging fruit and feed them to Faery or banish them."

"What about the question marks? The ones we're not sure of?" Titania quirked a brow.

I'd thought about that before and had a ready answer. "Some will leave Faery. Oberon will strongarm others because he realizes if he doesn't strike immediately, he'll lose whatever advantage he had."

"The stealth advantage is gone. Poof," Dariyah muttered.

"It is," I agreed. "What I'm still pondering is what to do about those who were on the fence."

"On the fence, how? In order for my former consort to compel anyone to carry out his bidding, he has to have something they either need or value." Titania crooked two fingers my way.

"Not necessarily," I replied. "Many of Faery's citizens have remained loyal to Oberon. He may have walked out on his responsibilities, but he never officially relinquished his position as liege. What could change their minds is this. By now everyone knows he was responsible for a unicorn's death. The unicorn who sits on the court will have made certain that little snippet was splashed far and wide. It won't sit well with any except Oberon's most hardcore proponents."

Titania's face settled into a mask of disapproval with lines carving through her cheeks and forehead and spiraling outward from her eyes. "I have news for them. Choice time is over. They will either leave Faery or donate their magic to her. No middle ground."

I turned to face her. "What about those who honestly believe they were misled? That they made a mistake? Oberon was their liege for millennia. Believing in him was ingrained."

"You're a strong regent." Titania's tone had softened. "You believe in your people."

I cleared my throat. "We've been making excuses for Oberon for as long as I can recall. Hell, I've made plenty of them. Up until his perfidy was so in-my-face I couldn't ignore it any longer, I was still trying to come up with ways to lure him back to save the land.

"Pfft. What a fool I was. Anyway, my point is if I could be hoodwinked, others might have been as well. The unicorn who died because of his treachery is likely to bring a whole lot of them to their senses."

"At some point, you will tell me about the unicorn. Meanwhile, we'll determine more once we're in Faery. How about if we play this one by ear?" Titania suggested.

I shook my head. "Not we, my queen. Once you take your place on Faery's throne, you will no longer require my services as regent." I sorted how I felt about it. Mostly, it was a relief. I'd still work on Faery's behalf, but without the crushing responsibility of her wellbeing sitting squarely on my shoulders.

"Nay. You shall remain as regent," Titania said firmly. "With everything we face, steering Faery's fate is too big a job for one."

"If my scrying runs true," Auril tossed out, "all four of us are required. I admit I lacked an identity for the fourth person until Cynwrigg walked into today's vision, but his magic is a perfect complement to ours." Power shimmied around her as she built a teleport spell. "I shall be in my old quarters laying the groundwork to resurrect my court."

"We will go to Dubrova." Titania nodded briskly. "It will be a pleasure to see my rooms once again."

Dariyah surprised me when she said, "I'll be along. I need to stop by Earth and check on my cat. He's been alone for a while."

"Surely, you can do that later," Auril suggested silkily. It was subtle, but I felt the zing of compulsion threaded into her words.

Apparently, so did Dariyah. "I could"—she batted away strands of her mother's transport spell that had begun to wrap around her—"but I'm not going to. Remember? My head is forfeit in Faery. Means I have to keep my glamour going full blast 24/7. I'm tired. My head hurts. My hair smells because it's burned. I'm going to clean up, give myself a haircut, see to Midnight, and then I'll find my way to Dubrova."

"But I hoped you'd come with me." Auril had dropped all efforts to control her daughter. What I read in her words was naked yearning and the pain of long separation.

Dariyah's eyes filled with tears. Where they fell, gems sparkled in the afternoon sunlight. She walked to Auril and embraced her. "I love you too, Mother. I'd never thought to see you again. Any time we have together is an unexpected gift."

Auril hugged Dariyah back and kissed her forehead before letting go. "I trust your judgment. Faery will alert me when you arrive."

I scooped up a handful of precious stones and handed them to Dariyah. "If you could use help," I told her, "I can finesse a quick trip to Earth once I've made certain Titania is comfortable."

She pocketed the gems and started to laugh. "Geez. I've gone from having no one who gave a rat's ass where I went or what I did to a hovering family. Middle ground would have been nice."

"Is that a yes or a no?" I pressed.

She stood taller. "Your land and people need you. I'll find my way to Faery when I'm ready."

"It's your land and people too," Titania said tartly. "You must not tarry, child. Faery needs you. Your magic is a perfect match to hers. 'Tis why she called you daughter of her bones."

"This has something to do with my unknown father, doesn't it? Dariyah pursed her mouth into a scowl. "Oh, that's right. Not so unknown as all that. Mainly, unknown to me." She waved a hand off to one side. "Don't mind me. I'm tired and out of sorts."

Now that I knew what I was looking for, I was halfway certain I could tease out who her father was, but Auril had been quite clear the timing wasn't right. My loyalties lay with Dariyah, but I trusted the Queen of Air and Darkness knew what she was about. Knowledge given too soon could prove disastrous. If her father was who I suspected, even thinking his name could bring him on a dead run. He'd been banished from Faery long, long ago. Unlike others who'd broken our laws, he hadn't skulked away. Oh hell, no. There'd been a dramatic, in-your-face battle. Scars from it were still visible on a faraway hillside in Faery's eastern sector.

I did not want to end up in the middle of a mess of my own making that might cause still more problems for my land and subjects. Dariyah slitted her eyes my way in such a manner it was clear she'd been privy to my thoughts and did not agree with the conclusion I'd come to.

Damn it. We needed time alone. A protected space where I could hold her close and restore the alchemy the two of us made together. "The safest path into Faery is the stairs leading downward from the casino," I told her.

"Thanks for the tip." Her inflection implied she neither needed nor wanted my suggestions. What she expected me to divulge was anything I knew about who her father might be, but it would be folly to fall into that pit. Besides, I could be way off base and kick a hornets' nest open for nothing. Light flickered around her. When it cleared, she was gone.

"I'll be on my way too." Auril grasped Titania's hands. "I've waited for this day, longed for it and feared it both. No matter which way the winds of fate blow us, we are meant to face this together, Sister."

"*This day* would have arrived faster if you'd not left Faery in the first place." Titania tilted her chin.

"Your opinions haven't changed. Neither have mine. Ensuring the child's safety was paramount. I wasn't at all certain it would have been possible in Faery. Now that you've seen her, felt her power, surely you agree."

"Not necessarily. The future holds many branches. Who can say which one would have unfolded had you selected a different path?" Titania retorted.

I'd fallen into an old argument, and one where there couldn't possibly be a clear winner. It was as good a time as any to intercede. "Ready to leave, my queen?"

She turned her golden gaze on me. "Ever the gallant. Do you still have a stable of women at the ready?"

My face warmed under her scrutiny. I'd been a bit of a blade in my younger years, but the allure of a fresh body every night had faded a few hundred years ago.

"Not exactly. You've been gone a while," I demurred.

"Not so long as all that," she corrected me.

"If you are interested in my daughter"—Auril had walked near enough to thump me in the chest with an index finger—"you will not dishonor her by—"

"Stop it, both of you." They might be queens, but I drew the line at their noses jammed up my backside. I glided beyond Auril's easy reach and addressed my next words to Titania. "What I did in the past is my affair, but I wouldn't have to work very hard to gin up a list of men—and women—who were bigger players than me."

After considering adding a jab about her pet satyr, I decided prudence was the better course and turned to Auril. "I respect your daughter. She's amazing and special. We're getting to know one another. I have no idea where things between us will go, but we have traitors to flush out and a liege to depose before anything personal will get much airtime."

I cobbled a spell to take Titania back to Faery. She glared at me. "I can manage on my own."

"I'm sure you can." I bowed low before straightening. "I will leave you as soon as I'm certain you've passed Faery's borders and are safe in Dubrova castle."

"Not necessary," she growled.

"Aye, but it is. Oberon knows you've escaped. He may have set snares, and it's a sure bet he's activated his network of spies. While you're more robust than you were when we found you on that other world, you still have a ways to go before your full power is restored. My plan is to surround you with unicorns and satyrs until we are certain what we face."

Auril closed her teeth over her lower lip. "Should I go with her?"

Titania shook her head vehemently. "Let's keep your homecoming a secret until you reconvene the Midnight Court. By then, we'll have a better sense of how deep Oberon's rot has cut into Faery's heart."

She strode to my side. "You make good points, Regent. Take us to Faery."

Relief washed through me. I'd been afraid she'd refuse because pushback about my youthful—and not so youthful—affairs had annoyed her.

"You know where to find me," Auril said and disappeared.

Before Titania could change her mind, I constructed a spell and launched it. My statement about her not being anywhere close to her full capacity magically had been kind. She needed rest, food, and the healing presence of Faery.

"I never did thank you properly for rescuing me," she said.

"No need. Actually, you were closer to the mark when you chided me for taking so long."

"None of it matters." Her tone was firm. "Our eyes are focused ahead, not on what is past."

It was especially true for her, but I didn't rub salt into her wounded places by saying it. Like all the rest of us, she'd cut Oberon slack again and again and again. Each time, he'd roared back to make her sorry she'd forgiven him. Being lord and lady of Faery had complicated things. Relationships came and went for immortals, but kings and queens didn't divorce. They might be estranged, live separately, but on the surface they were still a couple. And this particular couple had legends of their unbreakable love to uphold. I'd been raised on storybook depictions of their timeless romance. It hadn't been until long after I was grown I realized none of them were true.

It took longer than I'd expected before my casting developed grayish edges signifying we were nearly at our destination. "Do you have orders for me, my queen?"

"Of course not," she snapped. "Your judgment didn't evaporate because I'm here. Do as you wish. If it doesn't meet with my approval, I'll let you know."

"As you will, my queen." The words were automatic, but I hadn't cared for her message. Much simpler to have a direction in mind before I took a wrong turn—in her eyes. I'd been running the show in Faery for long enough to possess my own ideas about what the land and her people required.

After we'd both rested, Titania and I would sit down and hold a brutally honest conversation about the shared leadership she envisioned and how it would work. If her idea was giving me my head until I did something she disapproved of, we'd have to get a few things straight because I couldn't operate like that.

I opened a telepathy channel and summoned a few unicorns and satyrs, telling them to meet us in the chamber housing the court. The room took form in fits and starts, demonstrating how tapped out my magic was.

"Not the smoothest entry," Titania murmured.

"We're here, aren't we?" I sniped, followed by, "Sorry, my queen. It's been a long couple of days." Just because I didn't want her micromanaging me was no reason to be rude.

I blinked, bringing the room into focus. Titania slid from under the arm I'd had around her shoulders. Three unicorns and three satyrs bowed low amid a chorus of, "my queen," and "to your health," and "welcome back."

She stumbled, but recovered quickly. I hadn't realized how weak she still was. One of the satyrs pranced forward. "Lean on me, my queen. I will see you to your rooms."

"No need to lean on anyone." She stood tall and walked by his side as they left the courtroom.

"Thank you," I told the others. "Please post a guard on her floor. No one goes in or out unless they have an absolute reason for being there."

The unicorn who sat on the court nodded, mane bobbing around one side of his neck. "Where was she?"

"An outer world with guards who kept her from leaving."

"What happened to them?" a satyr asked.

"Dead."

He pawed the wooden floor. "Excellent."

"Something isn't right here," the unicorn said. "It's subtle, but the energy is off."

"Has anyone spoken with Faery?" I'd been rocking from foot to foot to counteract weariness.

"We were just talking about doing that," the unicorn replied. "Jess and me."

I glanced at my blood-and-soot-stained clothes. "Give me five minutes to change and slop down some mead. I'll go with you."

"Certainly, Regent." The unicorn touched my shoulder with his horn.

I trudged out of the courtroom. The energy shift could have something to do with Auril's arrival, except she couldn't have been in Faery for more than a few minutes.

Aye. That would have been an easy answer, my inner voice croaked. Damn, even it was weary.

I didn't remember climbing the stairs, but I was passing beneath the lintel into my rooms. I paused in the doorway, checking to see if my quarters had been disturbed. They hadn't. After closing the door, I dropped my filthy garments in a heap, walked toward the bathroom, and opened my magical center to Faery hoping for a quick infusion of energy.

The leisurely few minutes I'd anticipated where I cleared my mind and thought about exactly nothing weren't to be. Was Dariyah all right? She was a target too, and at the moment she was angry with the world in general, and me in particular.

Running on autopilot, I dressed in clothes that didn't stink of battle, retrieved my leather pouch of magical accoutrements from the trousers I'd discarded, and hustled downstairs to meet the unicorn and Fae. Jess had been the only Fae on the court who'd refused Oberon's inducements. I'd have to ask her what they'd been. It could offer clues about why Faery's king had been so hard to say no to.

CHAPTER FOUR, DARIYAH

My empty living room stretched around me, but I kept my travel spell open. Ready to bolt at the first sign Oberon's spies had infiltrated my new apartment, I scanned as carefully as I could, given my exhausted state.

My digs hadn't been disturbed. Or if they had, a master mage had been behind it and erased their footprints. My spell frittered to nothing; I sank into a cross-legged sit on the pale beige carpet. My head felt sludgy. It was tough to paste two consecutive thoughts together.

I should be delighted. Thrilled to be reunited with Mother. Instead, I felt empty, cheated. She was still treating me as if I were a child and she held all the cards. While I'd settled for my second-fiddle slot before, albeit reluctantly, I'd be damned if I would now.

What had I been expecting?

Nothing, since I'd assumed I'd never see her again.

Thoughts circling like a demented hamster running on a wheel, I couldn't come up with anything cohesive. Being back on the world where I'd grown up had hit me hard, but it was all emotions. A bewildering array of loss and need and love rushed through me as I evaluated my childhood and youth. Assessed through the lens of experience, everything was different. I'd loved Mother beyond wisdom or reason, respected her even, but I'd never liked her very well. She could be a bossy, dominating bitch.

"Ha. Guess I come by it honestly," I mumbled half to myself. If she'd been anything less than what she was, though, I probably wouldn't have survived to kick some serious ass myself.

Before I curled up on the rug and closed my eyes to get away from my unproductive thought pattern, I shunted everything aside and cleaned up. The burned spots in my hair had begun to grow back, so I didn't end up cutting off as much of it as I'd anticipated. It took me longer to locate scissors in the welter of belongings littering my living room than it did to trim my locks. Through everything, I felt as if I was swimming upstream against a strong current.

I needed time in the in-between place where I recharged my magic, but first I had to check on my cat.

Did I have enough magic left to conceal my presence? Midnight was at my old flat, a place Oberon had all but taken up residence. Maybe his attention would be elsewhere since he surely knew Titania wasn't under his control any longer, but I couldn't count on that.

My magic has a distinctive feel. If he'd hustled to the world he'd imprisoned his queen, he'd know right away Cyn and I had freed her. The more I turned it around, the less I liked it. Crap. Leaving Midnight in familiar surroundings at the old flat had seemed like a good idea when I did it, but I hadn't factored a raging king into the equation.

A raging king whose power is waning, I reminded myself. It should have made me feel better. It didn't. The shape I was in, the weakest hedge witch could make mincemeat out of me.

Whining isn't my style, so I finished dragging on clean khaki pants, a stretchy long-sleeved green top, and my boots. If I inhaled deeply, I could still smell blood and soot, but it was faint. No point looking for food. There wasn't any, but my old flat hadn't been particularly well-stocked in that regard, either. Besides, I wasn't hungry. The meal at Mother's was still digesting.

I built a ward and tested it. Not bad. If I didn't blow through magic teleporting, I should be fine. Not arriving in a blaze of power might buy me a few moments to get a gander at the lay of the land.

Unless Oberon was squatting in my living room like a reincarnation of Shelob. At least her carnage had been honest, not laced with subterfuge. Scooping up my phone from the floor, I glanced at it. Still half charged. I probably wouldn't need it, but bringing it wouldn't cost me anything. Scattering small bits of don't-look-here magic about, I left my apartment, rattled down a bunch of stairs, and set out walking across town. I had the Uber app in my phone, but the fewer people who could identify me, the better.

My Witch glamour was firmly in place, but it didn't alter my physical appearance, only my magical one. Night would be here soon. The day's heat radiated off buildings and sidewalks. It dawned on me I had no reason to remain in Reno. I'd moved here to make it easy to spy on Cynwrigg, but I'd never warmed to the place.

Winters weren't bad, but summers were ungodly hot, and there was nothing to hold me here. Should have thought things through before I rented the new place. My long-legged jog covered the distance across town in less than an hour. Sweat dribbled down my sides, but it evaporated in the bone-dry air almost as quickly as it formed.

I stopped half a mile from my flat and took to alleyways. Once I was alone, I clicked a ward into place and continued cautiously. I was still a couple of blocks away when the bite of Oberon's magic nipped me. Damn it. He was not only lying in wait, he'd set markers to alert him when I got close. I didn't think I'd tripped the one that just zapped me, not concealed like I was.

Ducking under an overhanging balcony, I considered my options. Could I lure the cat out from wherever he was hiding and sidestep stopping at the flat altogether? It was by far the best alternative. Too bad shapeshifting wasn't among my skills. I'd just turn into a cat and join the throngs of feral felines yowling from this corner or that.

It gave me an idea, and I crouched in shadows cooing softly. Cats are curious by nature, and it didn't take long before a parti-colored pair approached me cautiously. Was I something to eat? Or only the entertainment committee.

"Can you help me?" I kept my mind voice gentle.

"Mrowwww." One of the pair, a male, moved slightly closer.

Good. At least he hadn't taken off. If he was like Midnight, he wouldn't understand words, but images might get through. I thought about Midnight, holding a picture of him in my mind. Next, I used a subtle bit of magic to snatch up a mouse who'd had the misfortune of running past at precisely the wrong moment.

"Help me find"—I waggled the mental picture of Midnight—*"and I'll give you this."* The mouse dangled

between two fingers. Still alive, it squeaked its outrage. Live bait is always preferable to dead.

The cats touched whiskers, communicating in their own way. One took off like a shot, while the other remained. Probably to keep an eye on the mouse. It had managed to bite me a couple of times, but I'd hang onto it until I didn't need it anymore.

A deal is a deal.

Minutes ticked past. I'm not normally very patient, but waltzing into my flat and coming nose to nose with Oberon wasn't high on my list. Not in my current diminished state. I'd have to make a point of thanking Cyn for his transport services moving my few belongings to the new place. If any of my things had remained in the flat, I felt certain the Fae king would have destroyed them.

Displacement activity can be a bitch. Not especially satisfying, and you feel like a dick when you look at piles of busted stuff. Or maybe Oberon lacked any sort of social conscience. The more I rolled it around, the surer I was he hadn't felt badly for anything he'd done. Ever. Certainly not for the past few centuries.

The mouse had gone limp. Since struggling hadn't bought it anything, it was playing dead, but I wasn't fooled. The cat who'd remained kept angling glances over a shoulder. Worry for its companion streamed from the bundle of matted fur. I risked a barely-there beam of seeking magic.

Midnight's energy pulsed, but so weakly I jettisoned Plan A and handed the mouse to my kitty companion. On my feet, I glided silently closer to my flat. An image blasted into my mind, no doubt sent by my feline messenger. Midnight was huddled in one of his many hidey-holes. It had been sealed with magic, blocking his egress, and Oberon was slowly leaching air from the tiny space.

Fuck him. The bastard was amusing himself, not caring who he hurt so long as he could feed off another's misery. How in the hell had he become so twisted?

Anger began in the soles of my feet, adding vigor to my dwindling power. This wasn't a task for magic, anyway. Lucky for me—and Midnight—I knew my old flat well. Careful to maintain my ward, I hurried to the outer wall facing the back of the building. My cat had to be one of two places. Guessing right was critical. If I ripped the cheap siding off and missed my mark, the cat was as good as dead.

This close, even a subtle shot of power was certain to attract the Fae king's attention. Ick. It rankled to even think of him as a liege. What he deserved was a permanent end, soul separated from body, suffering the tortures of the damned.

Magic might not be open to me, but my senses are preternaturally sharp. I moved along the outer wall listening intently for Midnight's heartbeat. There he was. Still breathing, but noisily as he panicked at the decreasing air in his prison.

I couldn't risk telepathy to warn him I was coming, either. If he weren't so frantic, he'd have smelled me, but at this point probably everything magical felt like it was out to get him. The hefty tomcat would be a handful; I'd have to wing it once he was free. Building a hasty teleport spell beneath my ward, I readied it all but the last step. In one fell swoop, I dropped my warding, ripped a panel of cheap siding off the side of my erstwhile flat, and grabbed my cat.

Now that he had air, he yowled like a banshee, but my teleport spell was already engaged. Engaged, but slower than Hogan's goat to respond. Why? I had enough in my reserves to hop us out of here.

Midnight was hissing and scratching and biting. I couldn't spare magic to calm him, not when the alley wasn't exactly dissolving around me like it should.

"Come on," I gritted through clenched teeth and poured power into my spell. No more titrating whatever I had left. If I couldn't get out of here, it wouldn't bode well for me or the cat. Oberon had a prison all prepared. The spot Titania had vacated was available, and he could come up with guards to replace the ones Cyn and I had mowed through.

Not that Cynwrigg wouldn't come hunting for me. Or Mother, but I didn't fancy whatever torments the irrational king ginned up in the meantime. Midnight bit me for the umpteenth time. I set him down. At least he was free, and he'd know better than to let Oberon get within spitting distance again.

I hoped. My guess was he'd been sheltering in the flat, caught by surprise, and stymied when he'd attempted to escape.

Kitty took off like a shot duck. I'd try to find him later. If there was a later. He might decide to pick a mortal who led a less exciting life than mine. Or to take his chances alone. I wouldn't blame him. Either alternative was looking a whole lot better than hooking his star to mine again

Blood dripped onto the pavement from all the holes and gashes the cat had gnawed in my wrist and forearm. *Oh-oh*. Not good. My glamour may have survived intact; blood was a sure giveaway. I called it back, but I was a shred too late.

"You bitch," Oberon shrieked before I could actually see him. "Lying, conniving slut. Just like that mother of yours. She's supposed to be dead. Dead I tell you." His voice had become shriller with each subsequent word, and he stomped around the side of the building.

I narrowed my eyes, assessing him. He definitely appeared more ragged around the edges than he'd been before. "Mother's pretty hard to kill." I simpered sweetly. So long as I was on a roll, I ladled it on thick.

"She was thrilled to be reunited with her sister. You know, your ex-consort."

He growled and launched himself at me. I feinted left, counting on outmaneuvering him. Turned out I didn't have to.

My spell chose that moment to grow legs. Finally. Not dealing with the cat chewing a hole through my arm had given it the little bit extra it needed, and the place I'd stood fell away. Oberon's outraged curses followed me for a ridiculously long while. Cobbling together additional power to mask my trail, I beat a path to the in-between, the spot I refuel my magic.

Breathing as if I'd just run a marathon, I sank to my haunches and opened my magical center for an infusion of energy. Soothing darkness rose around me, cradling me in lush nothingness. At least I'd rescued Midnight. Another handful of minutes, and he'd have been dead. Fuck. His only crime was being associated with me. The Fae king's cruelty turned my stomach. Residual anger left me burned out and shaky, probably from the adrenaline rush retreating.

"Daughter!" Auril's sharp tones jangled my nerves worse than they already were.

"Yeah. What?" If my telepathy sounded as surly on her end as it did to me, she'd know how tapped out I was.

"We need you in Faery."

"Sorry. I can't go anywhere until my magic recovers." I'd

never have admitted it, but I was grateful for an excuse to zone out for a while. Too much had happened in too short a time span.

"We can't wait that long. Your power can feed off Faery's reserves."

A couple of neurons connected in my sluggish brain. I might not be jumping to Mother's commands, but she deserved to know I'd inadvertently blown the lid off one of her well-crafted secrets.

"Oberon figured out who, erm what, I am."

A long silence ensued, so long I began to hope Mother had focused her iron will elsewhere. No such luck.

"What happened?" she asked.

So I told her about the alley and the cat and my blood and waited for her to read me the riot act for being sloppy. She'd lectured me often enough about how being careless with my blood could bring ruin down on both of us.

What she finally came up with surprised me. *"He was torturing a cat?"*

"Yeah. It's what I said, isn't it? Midnight belonged to me. Oberon wanted to dick with me, so he hurt my cat. I'm glad I got there in time."

"I am too."

My eyes might have opened wider. Fae care about all living creatures, but in this instance, I'd expected

Mother to rebuke me roundly for expending my magic to salvage an unnecessary element, given the battles that lay ahead.

"Oberon is seriously warped," I ventured. *"I didn't think Fae ever acted like that."*

"Aye. He's been corrupted, and I fear it began long ago. He covered his treachery for an exceptionally long while, but whatever he sold his soul to has the upper hand now."

The idea some deeper, darker entity was in play left me speechless. But Mother knew things. Or interpreted her future-seeing and came up with possibilities.

My lungs had stopped doing a bellows imitation, but my magic had a long way to go. Or did it? I hadn't spent nearly long enough here for it to be close to topped up, but I felt stronger than I should.

Was this part of the blinders being snatched away when I'd set foot in Mother's realm? I was used to operating with a certain level of ability. If my skills had taken a massive leap forward in terms of the enchantment powering them, I needed to get with the program.

Maybe I would have had enough verve to take on Oberon. It sure hadn't felt like it, though. As I'd crept along the alley, I'd been sucking fumes, licking the bottoms of ashtrays, and hanging on by my toenails.

Mother hadn't said another word. Was she still in my head? A quick check told me she hadn't gone anywhere.

Suspicion scraped a hole in my magical theories. *"You're feeding me, aren't you?"*

"Of course. I already told you you're needed here."

"So I'm not any stronger?"

"They're not mutually exclusive. Use your imagination, child."

For some reason, it struck me as funny. I'd grown up hearing that phrase and hating it because it underscored my preference for the concrete, for what I could verify with my senses rather than flights of fancy. A snort of laughter escaped, followed by a whole lot more of them. Light and silly has never been part of my makeup, either, but laughing at myself was good for me.

While I was still chuckling, Mother's scents reached for me, enveloping me in the familiar feel of her enchantment. When it cleared, I stood next to her in a thickly wooded glade. My power might not be overflowing, but it had moved from inadequate to good enough.

I glanced around at bushes studded with richly scented white flowers that reminded me of plumeria. Tiny faeries hovered, their wings whirring so quickly they were nothing but blurs. Other small creatures from birds to mice to rabbits had formed a circle around Mother, jockeying to see who could get closest to her. Foxes and deer glided out of the forest.

"They missed you," I observed.

"Not them, but their great-great-great grandparents

and then some. Tales of the queen of the Midnight Court have been archetypal for the forest animals. They never gave up believing I'd return."

I pulled the tatters of my Witch glamour back into place.

"No need for that here, child. My magic will shield you from discovery."

I shook my head. "Not willing to take the chance. It isn't that I don't trust you, but I've been taking care of myself for a long time." I blew out a breath. "While we're on that subject, please stop calling me child. It's one thing when Titania does it, but…" I stopped there, at a loss for an explanation about why it was more palatable from Mother's sister than from her.

Today was one for surprises. She turned her silver gaze my way. "Aye, long past time for me to drop 'child' out of my verbiage." A fox was winding its sinuous body around her legs, and a doe had moved near enough to rest her head on Mother's shoulder.

"So long as you have the glamour up," Auril continued, "make a few alterations so we don't look so much alike. And then we shall be gone."

Her words spawned a spate of chirps and squeaks and caws from the assembled animals. The faeries fluttered near, stroking her hair with their tiny hands. "Not yet, my lady," one cried.

"Aye, you've only just returned," another called in a musical tones.

"I am not leaving the court again," she said firmly. "Tell your friends and associates the court will convene this night at midnight, and every evening thereafter." She lowered her voice. "Further, tell them they must not trust Oberon. If they see him, they should fade to nothing."

"Is it just him, my lady?" An owl clacked its beak.

"Would that it were." Auril stroked the bird's feathery head. "He has associates. We are working on ridding Faery of them. Meanwhile, exercise caution. Trust no one you do not know well."

"Where are we going?" I asked, but she placed a finger over her mouth. Probably wise. No one could wrest information from the animals if they knew nothing.

Poor Midnight. My next trip to Earth, I'd look for him, but make it clear he was free to roam where he wished. It wasn't looking as if I'd be in any position to make a home for him anytime soon, but I could buy him bags of kitty chow so long as we found a safe spot to stash it.

"Dariyah?"

Something about Mother's voice alerted me it wasn't the first time she'd said my name. Or my not-name. One more sore subject. "Yeah. Sorry. Ready when you are."

She hooked an arm under my elbow. "Slow and steady. It will sting when we pass the safety net I constructed around this spot, but it's kept the Midnight Court safe from discovery."

We walked forward. Not sure what to expect, I didn't exactly gird myself and bit back a yelp as current fried me. "Yikes. That was more than a sting," I groused.

"Eh, you get used to it."

She didn't tack "don't be a pussy" onto her sentence, but she didn't have to. We passed through three more invisible barriers, but they were gnat bites compared with the first one. Duborva's bulk rose in the distance. At least I knew where we were, sort of.

Cynwrigg raced toward us, flanked by two unicorns. Magic formed streamers behind him, creating a rainbow of possibilities. Whoa. He grew more profanely gorgeous every time I laid eyes on him. Or maybe being home intensified his striking looks. I'd have slowed and stared, gape-mouthed, but Mother hadn't let go of my arm.

"Has anything changed?" she demanded.

"Like what?" I aimed an annoyed look her way, all too aware she still hadn't told me jack about why we were here.

"Dubrova is closed to us," Cyn said without preamble. "And Titania is locked within."

My next action was pure reflex. Raising my mind

voice I called to Ysir. *"Titania has returned. Find her and help her."*

Shock vied with relief when his cracked, rustling voice responded immediately. *"Dariyah?"*

"Yes, it's me."

"Why does my queen need me?"

"Because you're both locked in Dubrova castle," Cyn answered him.

The connection crackled to nothing. Had Ysir, the ancient librarian, ended it, or had something more perverse intervened?

We'd find out soon enough.

"Brilliant." Cyn clapped me across the back.

"Would you expect any less from my daughter?" Auril broke into a run, heading for the moat.

Her praise, rare as blue diamonds, warmed me, but I could luxuriate in it later. The unicorns cantered after Mother with Cyn and me close behind.

CHAPTER FIVE, CYN

couple of hours earlier

A I'd no sooner left the castle to meet the unicorn and Jess in the courtyard when an unpleasant surge of magic prickled the length of my spine, making the fine hairs on the back of my neck stand on end.

The unicorn reared, pawing the air with his hoofs. Jess ran across the cobblestoned courtyard casting anxious glances at the castle walls. Made of glass and stones and wood and magic, Dubrova's very foundations appeared to be quivering, except it had to be some kind of optical illusion.

"Same odd power I told you about earlier," the unicorn whinnied. "This surge was a hundred times stronger, though."

I raced back up the steps to the front doors, expecting them to open. They didn't. That was a first. The castle recognized its own, and I was regent of Faery. Very well, if I needed to spell my way in, it could be arranged. I splayed the flats of my hands on the carved wooden doors and muffled a grunt as a shock rampaged through me.

The unicorn and Jess joined me. Having seen what happened, Jess extended her hands, power flickering from her fingertips. After cycling through a dozen "open" spells, she dropped her arms to her sides. The unicorn tilted his horn, prepared to jam it into the door, but I said, "No. It won't do any good."

"If I touch the castle, it will recognize me," he insisted.

"Nay, it won't. Not any more than it remembered who I am," I told him. "The castle is part of Faery. Oberon still controls the land and has extended his reach to the castle. There's no other rational explanation." Breath hissed through my teeth. "Titania is inside. He assumed she'd return to her old quarters. Damn it." I made a fist, but punching the doors would be counterproductive.

"You can't second guess everything he might do," Jess said gently.

"I should have foreseen this one, though," I told her and raised my mind voice. *"Titania!"*

The queen didn't answer. It didn't bode well. At all. If I couldn't warn her, she was ripe for a second plucking. Not that she wouldn't go down without a fight, but if she at least knew what was headed her way, she could launch a defense.

"Can Faery alert her?" The unicorn pawed the ground with a restless hoof.

"Worth a try," I said.

"We'll go," Jess told me.

"Good enough. I'll stay here," I told them. "In case anything changes, someone has to stand watch. While you're in Faery's realm, ask if she can get Titania out of Dubrova." Alerting her was fine and well, but moving her out of danger was even better.

With curt nods, the unicorn and Fae shimmered to motes of light, leaving me standing a couple of feet from the front doors. How in the hell could Oberon cause so much trouble? He'd always been a pain in the ass, but nothing like this.

Rocking back on my heels, I examined the doors with my psychic vision, hunting for clues that might encourage them to yield to me. Another shudder ran through the castle. Rocks clattered down, and the crack of windows breaking suggested Oberon's master plan might be destroying the structure with Titania inside.

Had he knocked her out again?

Surely, she wouldn't remain idle while tons of rock

and glass and wood buried her. It gave me an idea; I shielded my telepathy as best I could and called Auril. She listened to me, I'll hand her that much. Beyond acknowledging the problem, though, she didn't offer any encouragement or advice.

Why should she?

Faery hadn't exactly gone out of her way to support the force behind the Midnight Court. Or maybe I had it wrong. The land had provided concealment and shelter long enough for Auril to give birth. Perhaps it had been all Faery could muster. I wasn't doing much good staring at the main doors like a fool, so I wended my way around the castle and tried every other entrance.

With similar non-results.

The root cellar looked promising. At least I made it past the folding doors and into the underground room before the castle rebuffed me.

Where were Jess and the unicorn? For that matter, where was everyone else? This was the most deserted I'd ever seen Faery. Had everyone detected malevolent emanations coming from the castle? If so, they'd do well to lie low, especially after everything else that had happened.

Others lived in Dubrova. Ysir, the ancient seer and librarian for one. His servants should be inside, and the entire kitchen staff. Assorted Fae occupied most of the sleeping rooms on the upper two floors. Surely, some of them were in their chambers. Why weren't they clamoring to get out?

Tilting my head, I assessed the castle. Had Oberon turned it into a reincarnation of *Sleeping Beauty* or *Snow White*? With hundred-year sleeping spells hanging from the eaves?

He scarcely required a hundred years. Whatever mayhem he had in mind would unfold quickly if I was any judge of such things. I'd circled back to the main entrance. Placing my hands on the worn wood had been singularly unpleasant, so I let power flow from my fingertips and probed the massive doors. Far as I knew, Faery's regent had never been barred from Dubrova before.

"First time for everything," I muttered and kept on sweeping the entry point with short bursts of magic.

Two unicorns cantered across the courtyard and up the steps. "Where is Ulane?" one asked.

"He's gone with Jess to talk with Faery," I told them, wondering if something else had fallen off the rails. "Do you require him for something specific?"

"Aye. We were grazing in our favorite meadow, and the grass didn't taste right."

I drew my brows together. "Not right, how?"

The unicorn on the left shook his mane until it fluffed in the breeze. "No longer sweet. It held undernotes of rot."

"Poison?" My jaw muscles tensed as I waited for his assessment.

"We didn't think so," he said. "More like something trapping water in the roots until they festered."

"Is it every meadow, or just the one?"

The unicorn on the right lowered his horn onto my shoulder. "Apologies, Regent. We cannot answer that question."

I started to tell them to make the rounds of all their usual feeding grounds, but a burst of lupine, lemon, and brandy revealed Auril was close. Leaping, I twisted in midair and took off at a run with the unicorns on both sides of me. I should have been too sunk in problem-solving to react, but a trill of excitement speared me when I spied Dariyah next to her mother.

Had she rested enough? Was Midnight all right? I shelved my questions for later, hoping for some quiet time alone with her.

"Auril is back!" a unicorn neighed excitedly.

"Aye, I'd know her smell anywhere," the other one nickered. "Does it mean the Midnight Court will reconvene?"

"I hope so." His companion kicked up his rear hoofs.

"If anyone can fix the meadow, it's her," the first unicorn whickered.

All business, Auril planted herself in front of me and

demanded, "I came as quickly as I could manage. Has anything changed?"

"Like what?" Dariyah aimed an annoyed look her mother's way. It told me Auril hadn't been forthcoming about our earlier conversation.

"Nothing is any different. Dubrova is closed to us," I said without preamble. "Titania remains locked within. Probably others as well."

"She's not answering me," Auril muttered. "We have to find a way inside."

"Let's see if anyone else can hear," Dariyah suggested and shouted in telepathy with Ysir's name all over it. *"Titania has returned. Find her and help her."*

The seer's rustle of a voice responded immediately, shocking the hell out of me. I'd assumed since I couldn't raise Titania, I wouldn't be able to talk with anyone else, either. Stupid of me. I'd never been a wartime regent, but it wasn't much of an excuse. Or any at all. Whatever it took, I had to up my game. Yesterday.

"Dariyah?" the seer asked.

"Yes, it's me."

"Why does my queen need me?"

"Because you're both locked in Dubrova castle," I replied and waited. Just because he'd heard Dariyah was no guarantee he'd be able to hear me.

"I will locate her, Regent," he said, and then the connec-

tion frittered to empty air. Had Ysir, ended it, or had something malicious interceded?

We'd find out soon.

"Brilliant." I thumped Dariyah across the shoulders, not bothering to mention I'd given up on Dubrova's residents far too soon.

"Would you expect any less from my daughter?" Auril sprinted for the moat. The unicorns hustled after her with Dariyah and me close behind.

Crouched on her hands and knees, Auril was conversing with the serpents that lived in the moat. Half out of the murky water, they breathed steam all over her. I turned to Dariyah. "Oberon hated your mother because everyone in Faery loved her."

"Eh. Maybe so. The creatures I've met so far seem besotted."

I wanted to know how long she'd been in Faery, whom she'd met, but it could wait. "How are you?"

"Okay. Oberon nearly killed Midnight, but I arrived in time."

"Finally. A piece of good news. He must have hurried here right after that."

"It is good news, but I got lucky. So did the cat. What do you mean you can't get inside the castle?" She arched a red brow. Hoots and whistles and bugles from the serpents were escalating. Auril had moved into the water with them. They swam back and forth with her riding first one, and then another.

"It refused me entry. Dubrova is linked to Faery. Their roots run deep into the same rocky foundations."

Dariyah closed her teeth over her lower lip. "This reeks of Oberon. We assumed he'd catapult his attack into high gear."

"For once, we guessed right. When we freed Titania, it was a huge blow. He doesn't like to lose."

Dariyah's mouth twisted into a wry expression. "None of us do."

Auril vaulted out of the water. One of the unicorns tossed her onto his back with a combination of hoofs and horn; they cantered around the courtyard. The other one trotted over until he stood next to us. "Maybe she'll ride me tonight."

I'd never seen anyone on a unicorn's back before, but I held silent. Clearly, the Queen of Air and Darkness was in a class by herself. I called for Ysir again; this time he didn't reply. Dariyah mirrored my action. He didn't answer her, either.

The castle looked the same, but its magic was changing. No longer gentle and soothing, it had developed cracks and deepening fissures. "Damn. It looks like the rift did," I growled and gathered power intent on teleporting inside.

"What makes you think the castle will let you in that

way?" Dariyah asked.

"It might not, but I have to try."

Auril plunked down next to us; her hair was still wet, but the rest of her had dried. "The serpents are shoring up Dubrova's underpinnings. And they're calling the dragons." Enchantment formed a flickering nimbus around her tall, regal figure, turning the air shades of ivory and violet.

"I'm going inside," I said.

Auril slitted her eyes. "Mix your power with Dariyah's. It just might work."

"But Oberon knows who I am," Dariyah spoke up.

"What? When did that happen?" I asked as alarm sluiced through me. We did not need any more problems.

"Long story. I'll tell you later," Dariyah said.

"He knows part of who you are," Auril corrected her. "Part. Not all. Which is one solid reason for not telling you everything you want to know."

Dariyah showed her mother a mouthful of teeth right before her magic slammed into me. We packed a hell of a powerful punch joined like that. It had stunned me the first time it happened, and it just kept getting stronger.

"We're going to make a full circuit of the castle," I said. "Check for weaker spots."

"If we don't find any?" Dariyah asked.

"We'll still pick one of the sides rather than the front. The main doors have always been hotbeds of power. If I were Oberon, it's where I'd concentrate the bulk of my efforts to keep us out."

"I figured his main objective was securing Titania again," she said as we rounded a corner and checked the back wall.

"It's part of what's driving him," I agreed and scanned a sector. It felt promising, so I repeated my examination.

"What's the other part?"

"Why do you think he detoured to Earth?"

She rolled her eyes. "Pfft. I get it. He wants us to suffer. You and me."

"He always had a petty streak a mile wide. Check there." I pointed at the corner where the enchantment felt weaker to me.

Power flashed from her raised hand, and she ran it down the place the wall angled into itself. "Not sure about weaker, but this spot has a different weave to it. Shit like this is a hell of a lot easier linked to you."

"There's a downside," I warned.

She dropped her arm to her side. "Yes?"

"This is one instance where magic follows the laws of physics. For every reaction, there is an opposite one that's at least as strong. If our combined power gets us inside, well and good..."

"But if Dubrova rejects us, it won't be pretty." Her full mouth formed a come-and-get-me grin. "Living dangerously is my gig. Bring it on."

I focused our joined power into a teleport spell, aiming for my rooms. If anywhere in the castle would accept us, it would be there, a location I'd taken great care to surround with my personal brand of enchantment.

Dariyah gripped my hand. Good call. We did not want to get separated. "Ready?" she asked.

"Never readier."

I loosed our mingled magic, fully expecting the courtyard to disintegrate, replaced by the familiar walls of my chamber. Nothing happened.

"Give it more," Dariyah said as the nectar of her ability surged.

Moved by her trust in me—in us—I opened the gates and ran wide open. This time, the courtyard flickered and vanished. That was the easy part. Pain seared me as heated knives—or what felt like them—stabbed from all sides. I wrapped both arms around Dariyah, shielding her from the worst of the attack.

Breathing became difficult as the air grew thin.

"Fuck," Dariyah panted. "Same thing that bastard did to Midnight. Tried to suffocate him. I will not let that sorry sack of shit be the end of me."

"I second the thought." My vision was hazing at the

edges as I gulped for nonexistent oxygen. My lungs seized as I tried to breathe. Crap. It was like drowning, but without the water.

It gave me an idea. Usually teleport spells are all earth and air; I added water, floods of it, to the casting. At first, nothing changed, but then all of a sudden we popped into my rooms. Gasping and panting, we sounded like a poor rendition of old-time steam engines. The jabbing, piercing sensation had ceased as soon as we escaped the liminal space where we'd been trapped. I fully expected blood to be seeping from hundreds of holes, but the entire thing must have been illusion.

"You okay?" I stepped back from Dariyah and ran my gaze over her.

"Yeah. You?"

"Aye." I glanced at the door. "Want to see what happens when we try to open it?"

She flashed a grin my way. "Like I said earlier, live dangerously. Or not at all."

I laughed. "Go big or go home, eh?"

"Something like that. Let's see if telepathy works any better now that we've crossed whatever separated the castle from the rest of Faery. Try Ysir," Dariyah suggested. "Or I will. He's less likely to be monitored than Titania."

It was a damned good idea. "Go ahead. He likes you, which isn't true of very many people."

"Did you find the queen?" Dariyah asked.

"There you are," Ysir answered immediately. *"I've been trying and trying, but I couldn't raise you."*

"We were...stuck," I told him not surprised the liminal space had cut us off from everyone. *"Things are looking up, though. We're inside Dubrova. Did you find Titania."*

"Aye, Regent, but I cannot wake her. I've tried and tried. An unusual spell is hovering around her, but so far I haven't located an antidote."

"We'll be right there, assuming we can get out of my chamber," I told him.

"Have you come across anyone else?" Dariyah asked.

"Aye, my lady. They're asleep too. What in the goddess's name has happened?"

"Not sure," I answered him. *"This would be a good time to consult your lore books."*

He chuckled. *"I'm a step ahead of you, Regent. It's what I'm doing right now."*

"We'll be there as soon as we can." Dariyah cut the connection and walked toward the door.

"Hold up." I tapped the surface of the door with one finger. It didn't rear up and zap me. So far, so good. Since the electrical charge I'd been expecting didn't materialize, I deployed a thread of magic and instructed it to open the door.

"Mmph. We're a bit on the sluggish side, but we're still online," Dariyah muttered.

Modern nomenclature aside, it was my assessment as well. Once my door stood ajar, I heard the castle creaking and groaning around us. Something about the spells around my rooms had insulated me from Dubrova's misery.

"Slight change of plans. We have to free the castle," I said.

"What about Titania and everyone else who's comatose?" Dariyah asked.

"The two are connected. If we figure out what kind of grip Oberon has on the castle, and sever it, the rest will sort itself out."

"Are you certain?"

"No. But we could waste a whole lot of time trying to rouse Titania and have the castle crash down around us. Some of Faery's power is imbued in these walls. If the castle fails, it will make it that much simpler for Oberon to swoop in and wrest control."

"Mother thinks he's a puppet."

My head whipped around. "What?"

"She's convinced he's working at someone else's behest, and that his free will took a hike."

"But who?" I shuffled through possibilities and couldn't come up with any malicious entity who'd give two figs for Faery. We weren't exactly a piece of prime real estate for anyone who wasn't already here.

"She didn't say. I assume by then she'd already spoken

with you, and she was in an all-fired rush to leave the place she convenes the Midnight Court." Dariyah narrowed her eyes. "I'm convinced it's why she reached out to me. I was recharging in the in-between place when she told me I was needed here. She wouldn't take no for an answer."

"Your power seems normal," I ventured.

"Only because she topped it up. We can take pot-shot guesses at who Oberon reports to later. Any idea how to address breaking whatever has the castle in thrall?"

"Since I don't know what it is—or who's behind it— we'll start in the courtroom. It's the other place in Dubrova where my magic should be potent." An idea took root. "We're going to blow the front doors open, and then I'll convene Faery's court. Good magic, the power that shaped Faery from nothing, will triumph." I didn't add "this time," but the unpleasant truth was the more of our hand we displayed, the shrewder our adversary would become. We had to figure out who was behind Oberon's swan dive from Faery's liege to its tormentor. What had they promised him that would make him renege on his sworn duties?

"Hate to bring this up, but what if the doors are the only thing holding the castle together?"

"They can't be. The serpents are shoring up the foundations, and—" Bugling blasted my ears.

"Dragons!" Dariyah screeched. "They're here."

"Excellent. Let's do our part and pry the entrance free." Anticipating success, I raised my mind voice and summoned the council members. Ulane and Jess might not hear me, but I was banking on Faery knowing what I was about. We might not be linked, but the land understood whose side I was on.

We didn't get any pushback from the castle as we ran down many flights of stairs and crossed the great room.

"Yes!" Dariyah stopped a few meters from the main door and fist pumped the air. "We can do this."

Hell, yeah, we could. I stared at a visible spell spanning the door in multiple places. Apparently, the spell's owner hadn't figured on their handiwork being viewed from this angle. Either they weren't all that bright, or the strands were booby-trapped.

"Start at the bottom," I cautioned. "We'll clip one element at a time, and then wait."

Dariyah tilted her head to one side. "What if there's some kind of cumulative effect primed to blow up in our faces?"

"We'll sense it long before we get to the last one." Sending a beam of focused destruction, I clipped the bottom strand. A tortured howl, distinct from the ongoing moaning I'd heard ever since my door opened, filled my ears. Somehow, the bonds were tethered to the core of the castle's being.

"No choice," I told Dubrova firmly. "We cannot leave you prisoner."

The howls turned to shrieks as we clipped the next strand, and the one after that. Power clotted until the air turned a pearlescent yellow, marked with bloody streaks.

"Should we stop?" Dariyah asked.

Every screech was like a spike in my heart, but our path was set in stone. "No going back," I told her. "We're going to sever the rest in one fell swoop."

"Bold," she mumbled.

"One at a time isn't doing anything except brutalizing the castle." I had no idea what would happen if we broke the remaining cords all at once, but what we were doing was tantamount to torture.

"I'm moving to the top," I told her, "and cutting downward."

Light blazed from our hands as we mowed through the remaining strands. I closed my ears to wails of pain. Believing in magic is over half the battle, so I visualized Dubrova standing whole, Dubrova standing free.

The last band fell away, and the doors creaked open. Lightning crashed through the entryway. Thunder boomed. In the midst of it all, I heard Ysir scream, "What have you done, Regent?"

❧ *6* ❧

CHAPTER SIX, DARIYAH

Waves of wicked energy roiled through the spot where we stood. Keeping my feet under me became a huge challenge. I heard the old librarian yelling, but couldn't make out his words over the melee around me. If I'd had any doubts about the castle being sentient, they vanished in a heartbeat. Not only was Dubrova alive, it was fighting to remain so.

I could help with that, and I fed power downward, instructing it to shore up the quivering structure. The electrical storm that raged around us as it reached through the door had magic stamped all over it. Had we loosed it when we kicked the doors open?

Not the kind of boobytrap I'd have set, but effective in a bludgeon-y way. Almost as if it were trying to deflect our attention away from its real objective. As I cobbled and patched, I twisted my neck around hunting for Ysir. He stood off to one side in slightly cleaner robes than the last time I'd seen him. Arms extended, he chanted softly. Light circled him, twisting like a cyclone on crack and speeding up as I watched.

I wasn't familiar with that casting except to recognize it was a summoning. He was calling someone—or something. I'd been planning to ask him if his lore books yielded anything useful, but I didn't want to distract his concentration.

A tongue of fire shot through the open door. "Out of the way," a dragon trumpeted.

"No fire in Dubrova!" Cyn's voice rang with command. "Not now. Not ever." He unhooked his magic from mine and faced off against a green-scaled monster. The dragon was impossibly large and incredibly gorgeous. I remembered not to look right into his eyes, but their swirling depths held quite a draw.

Good for Cynwrigg. Someone needed to be in charge of this shit show. A unicorn shimmered into view, flanked by Jess, the only Fae on the court who'd remained true to Faery. When I peered through the smoky murk, I recognized the unicorn too. It was the same one who sat on the court.

May I borrow your body once again, my dear, rustled through my mind.

At least Faery was asking. She'd been careful with my physical entity last time, but it hadn't been a particularly pleasant experience. Which was putting a positive spin on things. Playing host to her rampant power had wiped me out. Maybe I was taking too long to answer. I felt her probing the edges of my body when she said, *"It will be easier this time."*

"All right."

The words had no sooner left my mouth than I was tossed from center stage to a back seat in a cavernous auditorium. I have to hand it to her, she didn't use one iota of my magic. When she raised her arms and began to sing in a haunting, evocative voice, it was all her. I felt her draw power from the bones of Faery. From the earth beneath our feet and the castle's bulk rearing around us.

My efforts at patching and cobbling Faery's hurt places were paltry compared with the array stretching around me as Faery used my body to facilitate her magic. I suspected she'd had a body of her own once. What had happened to it? Was its loss Oberon's doing as well? Somehow, an undertaking that grand seemed beyond him. He was linked with Faery; surely, it prohibited him from causing her harm.

I felt Mother before I saw her burst through the castle doors. The entryway was crowded. At least four dragons had lumbered inside, along with Jess and the unicorn. Ysir, Cynwrigg, and I vied for space, but there wasn't much. One dragon would have been a tight fit. The other three were arrayed down a long central hall. There'd been no more fire, but smoke, steam, and ash filled the air. If I'd been in control, I'd have been coughing, but Faery wasn't fazed by the smoke-filled air.

I should be paying close attention. Noticing everything Faery was doing to salvage her hold on her world, but my mind was wandering, treading in tired little circles. Panic forced my eyes, which had been sitting at half-mast, fully open. Faery meant well, but she was draining me to bedrock, not unlike what she'd done when she'd commandeered my power to heal the rift in her foundations.

It made no sense. She wasn't using my magic. So why was I suddenly shaky as a newborn colt?

"It's time," I mumbled, shocked by how weak my voice was. Faery didn't even hear me, but Mother did.

She was next to me in a trice. "You must leave now," she thundered.

My head that wasn't under my control, turned slowly and regarded Mother. "But I am not done."

"You're killing Dariyah."

Laughter rolled from my throat. "Oh. Is that what you're calling her?"

"It is. Keep her name secret. Keep her safe."

"Just a few minutes more," Faery wheedled.

"One. Make it count." I recognized Mother's tone. It meant action would follow swiftly for noncompliance.

Faery apparently recognized it too. After one of the longest minutes in my life when it felt like the marrow in my bones was melting, Faery withdrew abruptly. I'd have fallen to my knees if Mother's arms weren't around me. I hadn't felt her shore me up, but she was there. Not just holding me, but pouring magic into me.

"Breathe," she instructed. "Nice and deep."

"Did she finish what she began?" I slurred.

"Not quite, but it will be good enough for now."

"She didn't take magic from me. Why am I so depleted?"

"Mismatch of energies. You are part of her, yet not."

Christ. She may as well not have answered at all, if all I got were riddles. I forced my eyes to focus on Mother's face. It took effort before her familiar features stopped swimming in and out of view. It wasn't my imagination. She looked worried. "If I were you," she said in the barest whisper, "I wouldn't do that again."

"My head was clearing. "She had a body once, didn't she?"

Mother nodded. "Astute of you."

"How'd she lose it?"

"Eh. Story for another day."

Annoyance flickered, but it was feeble as dishwater just like the rest of me.

Cyn reached us. "What happened here? Ulane and Jess were catching me up, and we were helping the serpents construct wards around Dubrova's underpinnings, so this never happens again. At first, our task felt impossible, but everything fell into place out of nowhere."

"Faery stepped in," Auril said dryly.

"But how?" Cyn crooked two fingers Mother's way.

At a sharp glance from her, I admitted, "She may have borrowed my body again."

Alarm painted lines in Cyn's high forehead. He turned all his attention my way and examined me from head to toe; his magic burned where it scoured my depleted places. He was even less diplomatic than Mother when he said, "Do not do that again. Shore up the glamour. It has holes."

I was certain it did. That it was still present at all was miraculous. While being scolded rankled, in this instance I agreed with both of them. By the time I'd understood I was in trouble, I was too drained to make my needs known. Faery had done the same thing when she'd taken my magic to heal the rift. She'd sapped me but saved me at the same time.

It was all confusing as fuck.

My mind traveled in weary little circles. All this had something to do with her labeling me daughter of her bones, but I had no idea what it meant. Mother knew. Probably Titania as well, and—

"Titania!" I mumbled. "Has anyone checked on her?"

"Ysir is with her," Mother said. "I've been keeping tabs on them both. She's awake. The enchantment is dissipating."

"What enchantment?" Cyn and I asked with one voice. We'd suspected one was in play, but I wanted to know more.

Auril looked askance at us both before letting her gaze fall squarely on Cyn. "You remember Snow White and Sleeping Beauty. Of course you do. You knew them. And every other sleeping enchantment betwixt now and then. The same principles apply."

"But why employ them here?" I asked.

"Why do you think?" Mother countered.

"We assumed Oberon planned to kidnap Titania a second time," Cynwrigg answered.

Mother shook her head. "When Titania entered Dubrova, the link with Oberon shattered. His mistake was bifurcating people and land, jettisoning one and keeping the other. It's had odd consequences. Elements are still playing out, and I haven't been privy to the endgame."

Since Mother appeared to be in a chatty mood, a rare occurrence, I took my chances and asked, "Is she linked to Cynwrigg now?"

Auril shrugged and hooked a thumb to her right. "Ask him."

Cyn frowned. "I can't sense her specifically, but she's part of Faery, and all Faery's inhabitants are joined to me. Except the ones in the *Dreaming* Oberon shanghaied to do his bidding."

"Makes sense." Mother raked a hand through her hair. The *Dreaming* is its own entity. It's never been part of Faery.

News to me. From the surprised look on Cyn's face, it might have been news to him as well. The green dragon who'd blasted the castle's entry hall with flames lumbered over. Even with his wings folded across his back, his shoulders barely cleared the walls on both sides.

"Regent. The court is assembled and ready to begin."

I straightened, shaking Mother's arm off from around me. "Thanks."

"Don't mention it." Her acerbic tone was back in spades. She hadn't told me I was an idiot, but she didn't have to.

In my heart of hearts, I assumed Faery would have bailed me out once she recognized what she'd done. Maybe. Swept away by enthusiasm, she was intent on salvaging her integrity. I could have ended up collateral damage.

"I want to be part of the court." Faery's voice was insistent and insidious.

"You can watch through my eyes," I told her.

"Not what I had in mind."

"It's the best I can do." I huffed out a breath. "You nearly damaged me."

"But I didn't."

"Only because Mother stepped in."

Everyone was walking toward the court chamber. I assumed I'd be part of the assemblage. Until someone told me otherwise, I'd find a seat and aim for a low profile.

Faery was silent after my last observation. I wondered if she could use someone else's physical being. Or was there something about mine that complemented her power. Mother had suggested half of me matched up fine. Which half? Probably not the Fae one, or most of the mages spread around the long U-shaped table would have served better than me.

Titania sat at the head of the table. Cynwrigg dragged chairs over. One for himself, one for Mother, and a third one. Before I wasted much time or energy wondering who it was for, he motioned me over and pointed to it.

I shook my head. "I'm not part of anything."

"Aye, you are."

It wasn't the place to argue, and it would have

appeared odd if I'd refused outright. Too many people sat within earshot. I settled in the indicated spot.

Cyn brought an intricately carved wooden staff down on the floor. The accoutrement glowed with a soft blue light. Funny, I hadn't noticed it before. Side conversations fell silent. When he propped the staff against the wall behind him, it sank into the panels and disappeared, which would explain why I hadn't spotted it.

"First, I would like to extend a warm welcome to our five newest court delegates," Cyn said.

It had registered that the table was fully occupied, but I wasn't firing on all cylinders. Must have been the quickest recruitment and vote in Faery's history. Rather than five Fae, their replacements were diverse. One Fae, one Sidhe, one unicorn, a satyr, and a nymph.

"I speak for us all when I thank you, Regent," the nymph said.

"No need. Change was long overdue," Cynwrigg replied.

Titania rose to her feet. Cheers rippled through the room, but she waved everyone to silence. "I have returned. I shall not leave again. There is no way to say this gently. Oberon is our enemy. Any who cling to loyalty to him shall be banished from Faery. If they will not leave voluntarily, their lives shall be forfeit. One of our first tasks will be to weed out the traitors among us. Do I make myself clear?"

"Aye, my queen," echoed through the chamber.

Titania nodded. "My next point concerns my sister, Auril. She is also back in Faery. Oberon made her life miserable. She is to be revered and respected. Any action against her will be interpreted as an act against me."

Mother stood. "The Midnight Court will reconvene later tonight. As always, everyone is welcome. My days of erasing memories are over. My court will no longer be a secret, hush-hush affair. Those who come to dance and rejoice can do so openly."

Cheers rang out, leaving no doubt Mother had been missed. Obviously, I'd never been part of the festivities, but I planned to rectify that as soon as I could. Maybe Cyn would come with me. I'd have to ask him. We could do with a bit of dancing beneath Faery's skies.

"Which brings me to my last point," Titania said. "From today forth, Faery will have both day and night. I have spoken with the land, and she was delighted to comply. Oberon's perpetual daylight wore on everyone." She sat and looked at Cyn. "You shall continue as regent, and the rest of this meeting is yours."

He bowed. "Thank you, my queen. For now, the castle is safe, but we must be vigilant. Magic from our dragon allies funneled through their sea serpent cousins and shored up Dubrova's foundations."

I listened as Cynwrigg parceled out tasks. First and

foremost was banishing those loyal to Oberon from Faery. The list I'd nabbed from his cousin's mind had been long. Neither of us had been certain how accurate it was, but if all two hundred and then some were guilty, it would surely punch a hole in Faery's population.

"Do they get a second chance?" Jess asked.

"Aye, what if some of them are innocent?" a satyr asked.

"Use truth spells," Cyn told him. "If anything feels off to any of you, we don't need questionable mages here."

"May I speak?" Mother focused her silver gaze at Cyn. When he nodded, she stood. "Oberon is a pawn in this game. I do not have the full story, but I believe he was coopted by the Lord of Winter and what remains of the Unseelie Court."

"But we welcomed both Seelie and Unseelie Sidhe," Titania reminded her sister.

Mother snorted softly. "Some spurned our offer, Sister, but it was long ago, and you may have forgotten. The idea was...appealing. So appealing we looked past those who walked out of that long-ago gathering."

"Our problem extends beyond Oberon," Ulane neighed.

"Aye. My point precisely," Mother said. "From what I can ascertain, his usefulness is reaching at end point. It's possible the King of Winter and his associates will pull

Oberon out of the game. They didn't approve of him kidnapping Titania."

"How do you know this?" Cyn's tone was sharp. I didn't blame him. I wanted to know too.

"I've seen them in visions," Mother told the assemblage.

"Why didn't you return before now?" Jess asked.

It was a reasonable question. I waited to see what Mother would say.

"I had other priorities, but I was on the verge of returning to Faery when my scrying told me Cynwrigg and Titania and a Witch were headed my way. I waited for them to arrive mostly to make certain I hadn't missed something critical."

She wasn't in any rush to out me as hers. I should have been pleased, but disappointment flickered. If I was destined to always be a bastard stepchild, I'd live with it, but I wanted her to be proud enough of me to claim me as her blood.

I rolled my mental eyes. Pride had nothing to do with this. She was protecting my parentage to keep me alive. At least until the covenant was reworked.

Cyn hadn't been in my mind, but his next words mirrored my thoughts. "We will reconvene at this time tomorrow. At that point, I will have reworked two portions of our covenant. The first deals with cutting the wind from Oberon's sails. If he comes back, he will not be able to reclaim Faery's throne. Any objections?"

No and nay circled the room.

His nostrils flared. "Excellent. The next portion for you to ratify has to do with mixed-blood pairings and subsequent offspring. Such activities are currently punishable by death for the children and expulsion from Faery for their parents. I plan to strike that section of the covenant in its entirety. One of the reasons we're in our current mess was Oberon's ridiculous obsession with racial purity. If you scratch deep enough in most of us, you'll find other than our primary mageline. If anyone has objections, raise them now."

A satyr raised his hoof. He'd been the one admitting to a longstanding affair with Titania. "Would this be retroactive, Regent? As in would it apply to children already born who've been carefully sequestered?"

Cynwrigg's stern expression softened. "Aye. It would apply to all children born of such pairings, including those already here."

The satyr smiled. "That was the right answer."

Cyn let his gaze fall on each of his court delegates. "Tomorrow morning, be here at ten sharp. We will vote to ratify the new covenant and sign off on it. Unless something else happens between now and then, tomorrow's meeting will be brief."

"What are you planning to do about the Unseelie and

the Winter Lord?" a blue dragon bugled from where he stood toward the rear of the chamber.

The green dragon puffed steam and smoke. "We remember him. He is barred from Fire Mountain."

Interesting on two fronts. That anything related to winter would have an interest in the dragons' arid world in the first place, and that the Lord of Winter had managed to get himself banned from it.

"Refresh my memory," Cyn said.

"He stole from us," the blue dragon hissed.

It made perfect sense now. Only a fool pilfered from a dragon's hoard.

"That's right. It's all coming back to me," Cyn said. "I have no idea what we're going to do about Oberon's associates. There's no love lost between us and the Unseelie who snubbed our offer of amnesty."

"They've been doing a slow burn for centuries," Titania spoke up and narrowed her eyes. "I still can't believe Oberon would ally himself with those rotters."

"Seems like a perfect fit, a match made in heaven." Mother managed to insert acid into her words, but I bet she didn't have to try very hard.

Titania shrugged. "Stop worrying. I don't harbor any lingering soft spots for my ex-consort, but he never did anything where he didn't come out ahead. What could they possibly have that he'd want?"

"Promises of a Fae-only land?" I speculated.

"Probably as close as we're going to get," Cynwrigg said. "Unless anyone has other pressing business, I will split the list of possible traitors among you. Work quickly. Report on your progress when we come back together tomorrow."

He rattled off names. Each delegate walked from the chamber once their assignment was complete. In half an hour, the only ones left were the dragons, Cyn, Mother, Titania, and me. If Faery had borrowed my ears to eavesdrop, she'd been damned silent about it.

I felt the weight of Cyn's gaze. "You need rest," he said.

It was true. I did. The question was where said rest would occur. My power felt ragged, frayed around the edges, and I still felt guilty about Midnight. I should make a good-faith effort to locate him and at least offer him the relative safety of my new apartment and a huge bowl of kibbles.

"I'm returning to Earth," I told him. "I'll be back in a few hours."

"I'm coming with you."

My eyebrows shot up. "I'm sure I'll be fine," I said stiffly. "I might not be at the top of my game, but I don't require a chaperone."

"My trip has nothing to do with you," he murmured.

My face turned into an inferno as my cheeks must have gone a brilliant shade of red. Seemingly oblivious to my embarrassment, he went on. "I could rustle up scribes to fix the covenant, or I can use modern office equipment. I've opted for door number two. I'll scan and PDF and edit to my heart's content. Shouldn't take long at all. And then I'll make copies for everyone."

Mother's frank gaze had taken on tinges of amusement. "If you're back in time," she told me, "come visit my court."

"I'd like that," I told her about the time Cyn's magic enveloped us both.

"Are you good with starting at Lady Luck?" he asked. "You need to eat, and food's already prepared there."

"We both could stand a hot meal," I told him, more than ready to move on from my earlier ill-timed assumption about his motives.

"I was hoping you'd agree."

"Will you tell me about this Winter Lord?"

"The Lord of Winter," he corrected me. "Yeah, I will, but none of it is promising. Out of all the blackguards for Oberon to ally with, I can scarcely think of a worse one."

"Mmph. Maybe we should eat first."

"Pick your poison," he retorted. "I'm not sure much about the Lord of Winter sits well regardless of whether your stomach is empty or full."

"I still vote for eating."

The walls of his office on the top floor of the casino

came into view. "Good call. We will." He headed for the house phone. "What do you feel like?"

"Surprise me."

After ordering two of today's special—whatever that was—he settled into his worn chair and booted up his computer. I walked around and looked over his shoulder. My jaw dropped when he opened a document titled *Covenant*.

"No need to scan it?" I teased.

"Nope. I've made a few changes before this."

I chuckled. "You're a man of many talents."

He angled a glance away from his screen and ran eyes brimming with lascivious intent up my body. "The ways I'd like to surprise you have nothing to do with my computer skills. Or Faery's covenant. Or dinner."

I could have done a whole lot of things, but since I was standing behind him, I threaded my arms around his chest and inside his shirt, delighting in the hot silk of skin beneath my fingertips. When he leaned into my touch, I ran a string of kisses up the side of his neck.

Maybe not my brightest move, but none of our problems were going anywhere. If anybody deserved a break, it was us. We'd play a little. Just until dinner showed up, and then we'd get back to the serious stuff.

"Keep telling yourself that." Cyn's deep voice had developed raspy overtones; his words proved he'd been helping himself to my thoughts. Reaching around, he pulled me into his lap and crushed his lips over mine.

My glamour fell away; my magic sought his, and our combined enchantment rose around us, hot and wild and bursting with countless promises.

CHAPTER SEVEN, CYN

I'd had stellar intentions. I'd make the alterations to the covenant, share a meal with Dariyah, and hit the high points about the Lord of Winter and his band of Unseelie thugs. I'd wondered why in the hell anyone would be interested in Faery, but that bunch would siphon power shamelessly from my world. Because they didn't give a rat's ass about her, they'd keep right on feeding until naught was left but a husk.

Oberon was the lynchpin in their master plan. Without him to hand Faery over on a gilded platter, the kingdom wouldn't simply roll over. Titania had a good point when she'd speculated about what was in it for Oberon. Something had to be, or he'd never have agreed.

All my honorable intentions crashed and burned when Dariyah threaded her arms around my shoulders and teased my chest with her fingers. Heat ratcheted through me. My cock thickened, shooting to full attention. Her scent was mystical, thrilling, alluring as fuck. When she latched onto my magical center with hers, I was lost.

Tumbling her into my lap was easy. Kissing her the most natural thing in the world. And the most exciting. An overwhelming sense she and I were destined for one another, that our coming together had been scripted long ago filled me. It was whimsical, ridiculous even, but it refused to budge. Ysir knew more about foreordained events than me, but if he'd known Dariyah was my one true mate—a phenomenon rarer than hen's teeth in Faery—he'd been damned quiet about it.

Perhaps the problem was he hadn't recognized her at all. Her Witch glamour hid her magical roots, and—

The sweetness of her mouth, her peaked nipples pressing into my chest effectively ended my mental wanderings. Her upper body molded to mine; her legs draped across my lap. She kissed me back with a fervor twin to my own. Our mouths crashed together, separated, and joined over and over as our kisses escalated in intensity. She teased the inside of my mouth with her tongue. Iridescent streamers, courtesy of our conjoined enchantment, wrapped around us until the air came alive with sparkles.

She bit my lower lip. I bit back. The coppery taste of

blood added spice. I couldn't get close enough to her. I wanted to absorb her, all of her, until there was only one of us. My breath, when I remembered to breathe, had turned into gasping pants. Arousal had never felt so sweet, or so urgent.

I cradled her head in one hand, fingers threaded into her lush curls. The other rested on her hip, but the temptation of her full breasts was too much to resist. I slithered beneath her top and filled one hand with a firm globe, pinching and rolling the nipple between my fingers.

A low, guttural moan escaped her, and she arched into my touch. When she moved, it sent waves of sensation cascading through me. My cock was tucked into the space right above her hipbone and below her ribs. I rocked against her, and she wriggled around to sandwich a hand between our bodies.

When her fingers curved around my errant member, heat and need exploded. I pushed her top up and out of the way and jackknifed around to latch onto a breast with my mouth. My chair toppled over, and we ended up on the floor.

Silvery laughter filled the air. "Easier. This will be easier," she murmured as she kicked a leg over my hips and straddled me. Heat from her surrounded my distended member. She rocked and rubbed against me. I had both hands on her breasts now. They'd become taut and heavy as her arousal swirled around us.

Because we were joined, I tracked her excitement, experimented with what pushed her higher still. Her hands were splayed across my shoulders, and she bent and licked my mouth. I opened to her tongue, and the nectar of her kisses made me long for the impossible.

For a different world where I had no responsibilities to Faery or anywhere else. For a world where I could whisk her to another place and fuck her in a million inventive ways until we slept and woke to pleasure each other again.

She broke our kiss and pressed her forehead against mine. "Yes," she breathed, "I want those things too. All of them. Such a lovely fantasy."

Her hips moved faster. I repositioned a hand and gripped one of them, holding her tighter against my shaft. The additional pressure pushed her over the crest. I shared her ecstasy as passion swung her into a series of ascending waves. I'd never mixed sex and magic before, but I funneled fire and air into our bond and was rewarded by still more spasms racing through her.

Where her vulva sat atop my cock, the heat level intensified until I moved my other hand to her hips. With my fingers spanning her slender waist and the flare of her hips, I thrust upward and let go of any semblance of control. She licked my ear. "Yes. Come, goddammit. Now. For me."

My mind had turned into a lust-riddled swamp. Coming was the only way out, but relief would be temporary. I wanted the woman in my arms with a single mindedness not even immortality would make a dent in. My balls tensed, snugged against my body, and released in sheets of rapture.

Somehow, Dariyah had scooted down, undone my trousers, and was licking up jism. I'd been so sunk in desire, heart beating like an out-of-control metronome, breath whooshing from my lungs, I'd scarcely noticed until her mouth closed around my still-pulsing cock.

A man would have to be dead not to notice that.

I tangled my fingers in her hair as she cleaned me with her tongue. When she moved her mouth away, the place it had been felt empty. "There"—she sounded pleased—"got most of it."

Desire still throbbed intensely, but I could think again, and embarrassment rolled through me. I hadn't come in my pants since I was a lad.

Dariyah slid back up my body, rolled to a sit, and ruffled a hand through my hair. "We were in a hurry," she said. "We did good."

I laughed. "We did, didn't we?"

"Um-hum. I bet dinner's out there. I thought I heard a knock a while back."

"Usually, they bring it inside."

"Maybe they tried."

"Maybe so." Public, and semi-public sex is common in casinos. So ordinary staff don't bat an eye. They'd never walked in on me before, but there's a first time for everything. It might make me seem more approachable, not that I wanted them to view me as one of the boys.

Dusting myself off, I got to my knees and then to my feet. Before I tucked myself back away, I wetted a couple of washrags in my small bathroom and tossed one to Dariyah. By the time I was presentable, she'd carried our dinner inside.

I gathered her close and kissed her. She tasted of me, and it made me hot all over again. "Maybe next time, we'll find a bed," I murmured after I lifted my mouth from hers.

She winked broadly. "I was kind of hoping for a tumble on the grass."

"Midnight Court?" I quirked a brow her way.

"Isn't sex what it's all about?" she asked.

I cleared papers off my table and moved plates off the trays. Surprisingly, they were still a little bit warm. "What do you want to drink?"

"Whatever you're having."

I grabbed two beers from the fridge and sat across from her. Once we'd had a few mouthfuls of a delectable version of fettuccine alfredo with garlic toast and a crisp

Caesar salad, I said, "The Midnight Court is many things. It's a place for dancing and revelry, for giving thanks to the goddess who made us all, but it has a serious side too."

"Go on." Dariyah set her fork down and took a long swig from her beer.

"The Midnight Court is a joining, a reaffirmation of commitment to Faery and its inhabitants. Ancient legends suggested so long as it continued, Faery would never fail."

Dariyah snapped her fingers. "That's it, then."

"That's what?"

"The reason Oberon hated Mother and drove her court out of plain sight. He wanted it to die to pave the way for his plans to sabotage Faery."

When she said it, it was so obvious, I couldn't believe I hadn't connected the dots before now. I'd assumed he was jealous of Auril's close relationship with Titania. Some men are like that. They can't stand their wives bearing allegiance to anyone but them. It's improved as the world has aged, but Oberon is old beyond reckoning. In the era he came into power, wives were possessions, chattel, no matter how powerful their magic might be.

I almost felt sorry for him. Almost. Embracing change was complex when it eroded power you felt certain was rightfully yours.

"Don't waste your pity," Dariyah growled.

"I won't. He's had many chances and blown every one of them."

"Tell me about the Winter King."

I drained my beer and got up for another for us both. The Unseelie court was unsettling enough, minus the King of Winter. After I was settled again, I said, "You probably know some of this history. If you do, stop me."

"I will. Go on."

"Long ago, Faery had four courts that bore the names of the four seasons. Titania and Oberon presided over the spring and summer courts. Auril and the King of Winter oversaw the autumn and winter courts."

Dariyah's eyes widened. "Mother was aligned with him?"

I nodded. "Aye, but it was very long ago. All of us shared this land until we couldn't. Our life views were diametrically opposed, and the strife was killing Faery. Every Unseelie raid to dismember mortals and suck their essence intensified the discord."

"Ewww. Mother mentioned something about that, but neglected to sketch in details about her role." Dariyah shook her head. "Faery's current problems aren't her first, then?"

"Nor her second." I offered a small, sad smile. "That Faery has remained whole speaks to her tenacity and her spirit. Your mother wasn't a willing participant in the

Unseelie raids. When they grew more frequent, she parted ways with the King of Winter and joined Titania and Oberon. Some said the King of Winter never recovered from the loss of his consort. For a time, he remained, but then he gathered a group of Unseelie loyal to him and disappeared."

I picked at my salad before continuing. "It was a relief to see him go. He was petty, cruel, and sadistic. When he wasn't killing mortals, his other favorite pastime was spreading lies to get someone stirred up. Once his latest victim raced away to confront the supposed offender—who was clueless—a fight to the death often ensued."

"With the king on the sidelines laughing about it, I suppose," Dariyah muttered.

"Aye. He thought it great sport. We dragged him in front of the summer court so many times I lost count, but he always had one excuse or another. His acts became even more reprehensible once your mother parted ways from his court and formed her own. When Danu offered her blessings, it was the final straw. Oberon wasn't pleased, either, but the Lord of Winter finally decamped.

"None of us looked for him. Hell, none of us thought about him. We were all relieved to be out from under the stench of his presence. Wherever he went, slime and misery followed."

"What happened to the other Unseelie?" Dariyah asked.

"The ones who didn't go with him, gradually incorporated themselves into the summer court. Oberon wasn't especially kind or accepting because they were mostly all Sidhe." I blew out a tight breath. Knowing our history and reliving it turned out to be rather different.

"What is it?" Dariyah placed a hand over one of mine.

"Faery has been in trouble for a long time. I've underplayed the seriousness of things because they were inconvenient. It's scarcely an excuse, but for every unpleasant occurrence, it wasn't tough to locate something positive."

"Mmph." Dariyah angled her head to one side. "Filling in the blanks, I'm going to guess Oberon kept in touch with the Winter King."

"Probably so," I agreed.

"Do you suppose Titania knew? Or Mother?"

I shook my head. "If they did, they'd have said something." I moved back to my computer and woke it from sleep. As I'd predicted, it didn't take long before my printer was whirring and shooting out enough copies of the revised covenant for the court to review and approve.

Dariyah started stacking our empty plates.

"No need to do that," I told her.

"It's a habit. I don't like leaving messes. I'm going to make an effort to locate Midnight. If he's findable, he'll be with the pack of feral cats roaming my old neighborhood."

"If you wait a moment, I'll come with you."

An impish grin made her look about fifteen. "I thought your trip to Earth wasn't related to me. At all."

I met her green-eyed gaze. "If you'd rather go alone, I understand."

"That's the problem"—her voice was soft—"being with you makes me never want to be alone again, and it scares the hell out of me."

Her words arrowed deep into my soul. I blundered around, picking and discarding what to say, and finally settled on, "I get it." There was more, so much more inside my heart, but we were quite new. I didn't want to make assumptions or create the burden of expectations too soon.

You're a craven bastard, my inner critic observed.

I didn't bother to answer him as I got up and walked to the printer. Scooping pages from its tray, I chucked them into an old leather briefcase.

She looked me up and down, frank in her addition of magic and thought-thievery. A spell built in the air around her. I walked close enough for it to envelop me too and heard her mutter, "Glad I'm not a dude," before the casino disappeared, replaced by a seedy neighborhood.

"Makes two of us," I teased. "Did anything in particular spawn that thought?"

She gave me a quick hug. "Yup. You're scared of commitment too, but you'd die before you'd admit it."

"Guilty as charged. But see? You can read my mind, so I don't have to talk." I kissed her forehead and let her go.

She mock slugged my arm. "Wimp."

"But a wimp who cares about you." I added a pithy point of clarification.

We got lucky. It wasn't dark yet, and neither of us had constructed a ward. No one saw us pop out of nowhere. I'd have heard screams if they had. Dariyah padded toward the far end of a smelly alley with several overflowing garbage bins. Sure enough, I sensed prowling felines. They'd hidden themselves once they knew we were nigh.

Humans might have missed our sudden appearance, but cats miss very little. Dariyah sank into a crouch and mixed words and a low crooning. Kitty heads peered from around heaps of trash.

A brisk *mrowww* was followed by Midnight's dark form streaking into Dariyah's arms. "You're all right," she murmured, holding the cat close. "Thank the goddess."

They cuddled for long moments before Dariyah sent

a series of images into the cat's head. She was asking what he wanted to do. If he was satisfied remaining here on his own, or if he wanted to be with her.

He sent mind pictures back. His were of mice and rats and kitty food dishes. She switched to words. "Yes to all of the above, but not so much as here. I won't be there all the time, but I'll build you a kitty door so you can come and go. Or leave a window open."

He lifted his snout and licked her neck. I could hear him purring from where I stood off to one side. Damn Oberon's eyes. How could he have harmed such a creature? And then it dawned on me it hadn't been Oberon at all. Well, it had been, but his will wasn't his own. Torturing animals was right up the King of Winter's alley. The implication was staggering. Auril had said Oberon was being piloted by another, but I hadn't absorbed the extent of what it meant until this moment.

Dariyah stood with the cat still firmly in her arms. "Let's go to the other place."

I nodded and constructed shields on top of shields to ward our passing. I hadn't looked for Oberon's minions —or the King of Winter's to put a finer point on it—but neither was I taking any chances. The walls of Dariyah's empty living room rose around us.

"There's a store not far from here," I said. "Want me to buy cat food?"

"That would be wonderful. Any kind will do. He's not picky."

A quick, non-magical trip out her door and down her steps landed me at a Quick Stop. I snagged two bags of kibbles, canned tuna, and a few tins of cat food and was back with my bounty in a few minutes.

Dariyah sat on the floor, still holding her cat. He yowled at me. I got the picture and fished a bowl out from the mess of Dariyah's belongings still scattered through the room. Midnight had liked tuna before, so I dumped a can into the bowl and set it next to a wall in the kitchen. When I looked under the sink, I came up with a dishpan and filled it to the brim with water.

Midnight squirmed out of Dariyah's embrace and raced to his unexpected treat. "How's he going to move in and out of here?" I asked. "The windows are pretty high off the ground."

"Not on the stairwell side." She got to her feet and cracked a slider just wide enough for the cat, sealing the track with magic to ensure no one could pry it open any farther. "Might be a good time to leave," she said, "while he's occupied."

"Does he know you might not come back?" I asked softly.

"I told him I'd do the best I could." She closed her teeth over her lower lip. "We can't move him to Faery, huh?"

"He wouldn't survive there," I said.

"At least I feel better than I did. He has a safe spot and food."

"Should we open the kibble bags?"

She laughed softly. "He can chew through them. And the cans in a pinch. No worries. He's resourceful. Come on. I'm just being overly maternal."

I built a spell and took us to the stairwell beneath Lady Luck. I wasn't certain of our next steps, and I wanted thinking time. We'd no sooner crossed the boundary into Faery than I felt the wrongness. It didn't take much digging to discover my bond with Faery's people was no more.

"What's different?" Dariyah asked.

"I'm no longer regent." I started off in a different direction than I'd planned on.

"But how?"

"My first guess is Oberon returned and claimed kingship as is his right."

"Nooooo. That's horrible. Where are we going?" Dariyah hissed.

"Not Dubrova."

"Okay. So that's where we're not going." She spun one hand in a come-along motion.

I shuffled through options, not seeing very many, and shuttered my magic. I did not want to alert anyone I'd crossed Faery's borders. Gripping Dariyah's hand, I said, "Ward us. Make us invisible."

"Done."

"We're going to find Auril," I said.

"And then what?"

"And then we plan a full-scale war. I'm done with Oberon bouncing in and out of here like a windup toy."

"We'll get him," she said.

We had to. If we didn't, everything good and pure in Faery would shrivel and fade to nothing while the Unseelie grew fat on her magic. That wouldn't happen. Not on my watch, and not ever if I had a say in the matter.

I might lack a link to anything, but I'd find a way around it.

8

CHAPTER EIGHT, DARIYAH

This had to be a desperate gambit on the King of Winter's part. All his careful plans to waltz in and take over Faery—via his puppet, Oberon—had fallen apart when they failed to take possession of the castle. The dragons showing up had been a nice touch, and probably a hell of a wakeup call.

If the Unseelie lord was going to make a move, he had to act quickly. So he'd trotted Oberon back into Faery to pick up the reins as if he'd never left. Could the court still veto his return, absent having ratified the new covenant?

A thought slammed into me. "Have them lie," I muttered as we loped through Faery, heading for Mother's domain.

Cyn glanced at me. "Have who lie?"

"The court. Can't they backdate the new covenant or something?"

"I don't like asking them to do that," he said slowly, "yet it may be the simplest way out of this."

"Tough to prove it's not true," I pressed. "Earlier, the delegates agreed on your two additions. The way I see it, them signing off is a formality. The discussion's already happened."

Cyn chuckled. "You should have been a lawyer."

"Perhaps someday I will be. It beats spying on cheating spouses."

"Or reluctant regents?"

"That too." I laughed.

The ambience of Faery flowed around us, but with subtle alterations in the weave of its magic. It felt like the leading edge of disaster, but maybe I was overreacting because I knew too much.

"Is this Winter King person part of the Shadow Kings?" I asked.

Cyn skidded to a halt and placed a hand over my mouth. "Ssht. Do not mention them. Particularly not here, but nowhere is safe. How do you even know about them?"

His reaction surprised me. "Mother mentioned them in passing. I'm the bastard stepchild, remember? Still working on figuring out how stuff slots together."

Grasping my hand, Cyn started forward again. "They

were a band of hoodlums who broke from the Wild Hunt and formed their own power base. There was a time they could bend the astral plane to their will—and close off gateways between worlds at their pleasure."

"But not anymore?" I probed. Sheesh. How much evil stalked the world that I didn't know about?

"No one's had a run in with them since the Dark Ages," Cyn replied, "but they haven't gone anywhere. And we'd better hope the King of Winter hasn't joined forces with them."

"Because it could close us off from Earth or Faery," I murmured.

"And everyplace else too."

"Maybe Mother will know something."

Cyn angled a wry look my way. "Knowing and sharing don't always go together."

Ain't that the truth, particularly with Mother. I got my bearings. We weren't far from the glade where she'd pulled me into Faery. When I scented the air, her unique blend of lupine, lemon, and brandy teased my nostrils. A shimmery corridor formed around us with a definite pull.

"Appears Auril is in a hurry," Cyn observed as the vortex doubled our forward momentum.

"She's always in a hurry," I retorted, "but in this case it appears justified."

"More than justified." Mother's rich voice reached

me before she hustled into view. She'd changed from the cobbled-together clothing, that was all I'd ever seen her in, to dark brown leather pants and a tunic that fit her like a glove. Painted with blue and green runes, the garments had to be left over from when she'd lived here. The leathers looked new; she must have spelled them comprehensively, or they'd have rotted away long since.

"I've been dithering about hunting you down," she said. "I tried telepathy—several times—but couldn't reach either of you."

"Doesn't work very well between Faery and Earth," Cyn noted dryly.

Mother rolled her eyes. "Eh. Probably not. I've been gone a while. Not that it worked before I left, either, but..." She shook her head briskly. "We have problems."

"Oberon's back, isn't he?" Cyn arched a fair brow.

"He is, indeed. And claiming kingship rights. He's taken up residence at Dubrova and has stationed armed guards at all the entry points."

"If they're part of the squad he woke from the Dreaming, they're not much of a threat," Cyn said.

Mother shook her head. "Wouldn't that be nice. This bunch are Unseelie warriors. I remember a few of them. And they remember me as the one who abandoned their king."

"Where's Titania?" I asked.

"With Ysir. I've been expecting them to show up here for the past hour."

Trying to read between the lines of Mother's communication has always been a challenge. She was worried, but how worried? "Are you certain they escaped the castle?" I asked.

"Nay. I'm not. They're not answering me, either."

"Have you asked Faery?" Cyn blew out a breath.

Mother glanced my way. "She likes you. How about if you do that?"

"Sure. Can I do it from here?"

Even though I'd agreed, my last interaction with her hadn't gone all that well. After she'd nearly siphoned my power to fumes—for the second time—she'd demanded another go round controlling my body. I'd put my foot down. For all I knew, she'd written me off. Not many mages told the land no.

"It's either from here, or one of us is going with you," Cynwrigg said. A possessive fierceness ran beneath his words. It thrilled me and pissed me off. Hell of a mix of feelings. Was I going to turn into one of those females I'd always despised? The ones who longed for a man to take over and tell them what to think?

"Agreed." Mother's tone was terse.

I looked from one to the other of them. Piled on top of Cyn's protectiveness, Mother's went a step too far. I corralled my anger, reined in hot words, and took a couple of steps away from both of them.

Taking care to disentangle my skills from Cyn and the magical tractor beam Mother had used to drag us here, I kicked my mind voice open and called for Faery.

She didn't exactly answer, but a hollow feel to my telepathic sending suggested she was at the other end listening. I shelved my annoyance at her assumption I was free for the asking to meet her needs. I'd never been a magical land, and her actions probably weren't as high-handed as all that.

"Can you still talk with me?" I asked.

A nearby tree rustled despite there not being any wind.

Running on instincts, I snatched up a handful of rocks and placed them in a row. *"Move one if the answer is yes. Two if it's no,"* I said.

Two rocks pitched forward a couple of inches.

"Good news and bad," I told Cyn and Mother. She can't speak with me directly anymore, but I've worked out a primitive communications system.

"Are Titania and Ysir with you?" I asked next. The same two rocks rolled back to their starting place.

"Do you know where they are?" This time a single rock rocked forward.

I cast a sidelong glance at Mother and gave a small shrug. She said, "I've been listening to your questions. If it has to be yes-no answers, let's run through a list of possible locations."

Sounded good to me. *"Are they still on Faery?"* One rock moved.

Mother huffed out a tense sounding breath. She'd probably been concerned Oberon had shunted her sister somewhere no one would ever find her.

"Narrows it down," Cyn said and fed me a list of possible locations. After the first few, when it was clear Faery could also hear him, I nodded at him to pick up the banner. Not much reason for him to tell me, and then for me to ask her after she'd already responded to him.

Listening to the long list of names that presumably represented villages and hamlets, I wondered how many creatures lived here. More than I'd thought, for sure. It took forever before Cyn's query yielded a single rock in response. He and Mother exchanged anxious looks.

"Where is Nemia?" I asked.

"Beneath the sea," Mother said.

"Well guarded," Cyn added.

"By whom?"

"It used to be sea serpents, but my bet is Oberon traded them for Unseelie water sprites."

"Doesn't sound all that ominous," I ventured.

"Don't get tripped up on the term sprite," Cyn growled. "They're actually more like gnomes with long sharp teeth and no conscience. They absorb souls. It's how they feed themselves."

"What do we do first?" I asked.

"I'm going after Titania and Ysir," Mother said. "I'll bring a serpent or two along, but I'm thinking it's more of a one-person operation."

"I'll convene a special session of Faery's court here," Cyn said. "We can ratify the new covenant, and then go to work booting Oberon out of Dubrova castle. And his Unseelie guard with him."

"If he's so determined to rid Faery of everyone who isn't Fae, where do the Unseelie come in?" I asked.

"Two choices," Mother replied. "Either he's playing them and has a plan to kill them once they've served their purpose—"

"Or he's their tool and once they're finished with him, they'll drop him by the wayside," Cyn finished her thought.

"As far as he's concerned"—I spoke slowly—"it has to be door number one. He can't realize they've perverted his will. No matter what the payoff, he'd never have agreed with being reduced to a subsidiary role."

"True enough." Cyn frowned. "He might be an ass, but he's stubborn and full of pride. If he was aware his actions were perpetrated by someone else, he'd rip the world asunder to free himself."

"If the two of you leave here, let one of the owls or

ravens know where," Mother said as the air turned shiny and liquid around her.

"We won't go until you return," Cyn said and switched to telepathy as he summoned the delegates to the Midnight Court.

"I hope she'll be all right," I mumbled. Worrying about Mother was something new. I'd always viewed her as invincible, unbreakable. Perhaps she was, but I'd lived long enough to see plenty of magic go sideways.

"Do you want to join her?" Cyn turned to me, searching my face with his burnished metal gaze.

"Maybe. If you're sure you don't need me here."

He placed his hands on my shoulders. "Dariyah, I always prefer it when you're next to me, but the court will assemble soon. Oberon can't be two places at once. Even if he figures out I've called the court into session, the worst that can happen is him showing up and ordering us to disband. By then, we'll have signed off on the covenant."

Two unicorns cantered into the glade, followed by Jess and the other Fae. In the space between two breaths, the entire court had materialized. Most on foot, but a couple teleported. Concern for Mother nagged, so I leaned close to Cynwrigg. "Yeah. I'm going to track Mother. Hopefully, we'll return soon."

He nodded and clapped his hands. The court

quieted, and he said, "Unless anyone has any objections, we ratified the new covenant yesterday."

"Perfect." A satyr stamped his hoofs. "Just what we were going to suggest."

"Aye," a nymph chimed in. "We agreed yesterday. The signing is a formality." She hovered close and Cyn handed her sheets from his battered leather case to distribute.

Grateful the court was in a cooperative mood, I drew power to both track Mother and teleport to where she'd gone.

"Where are you going?" a unicorn asked me.

"She's joining Auril," Cyn answered for me. "Titania and Ysir are prisoners in Nemia, and Auril left to free them."

"But it's guarded by sea serpents," the same unicorn pointed out. "Surely, they wouldn't imprison anyone."

"They've probably been replaced by Unseelie sprites," Cyn told him, "which brings me to our next matter of business..."

The signed documents were floating back to him when my spell took over, sweeping me away from the glade. Tracking Mother was straightforward. I'd spied on her so many times growing up, it had become a game. How close could I get before she knew I was there? It had turned out not very.

Some things never change. I was still swathed in my

teleport spell when Mother's voice floated through my mind. "Bring more serpents. Dragons too, if you can locate any."

I altered the coordinates in my casting; the murky waters of the castle moat closed around me. I'd never tested my powers breathing underwater, but I trusted my skills would give me what I needed. A gaggle of serpents were huddled on the sandy bottom, half covered by a layer of muck and slime. The water was so thick with strands of gunk, it was tough to see.

"Auril says she requires more of you," I told them. *"Dragons too, if we can manage it."*

One of the serpents flicked his tail around, turning in a partial circle until he faced me. His scales were black with gray edges. Maybe they'd always been that shade, but it might mean he was old beyond imagining.

"And you are?" His tongue flicked out.

His question caught me by surprise; I floundered about for an answer. Of course, he'd want to know something so basic. While I was asking on Auril's behalf, I wasn't her. If my glamour was holding up—and there was no reason it shouldn't—he figured a Witch had dropped in on them.

Not many Witches in Faery. Particularly not in the moat issuing orders. This was where the rubber met the road. The revised covenant was signed and sealed. Part of its new wording dismissed the death sentence sitting over my head.

"Answer me or leave," the serpent thundered, not bothering with telepathy. Apparently, his vocal cords worked fine under water.

I took a chance, a big one, and jettisoned my glamour, funneling the magic that had powered it into the teleport spell I hadn't ever let go of. Not that I could escape quick enough to evade a herd of serpents with their superior maneuverability underwater, but I'd give it a good faith effort.

It beat hanging around while they tried to kill me for being an abomination.

The serpents formed a circle around me. So much for running away.

"That is one answer"—the serpent didn't sound nearly as foreboding—"but I require words as well. Who are you?"

He might be able to speak underwater, but I couldn't. I planted my feet in the muck beneath me and rolled my shoulders back. *"My name is Dariyah. I am Auril's daughter."* To make certain they were up to speed, I hurried on. *"The covenant has been revised. My life is no longer forfeit here."*

Another serpent laughed. Bubbles rose above his scaled head. "Least of our concerns."

"Rumors of your birth reached us long ago," another said.

"Aye, we discounted them, since the dragons couldn't locate Auril," the first serpent told me. He touched my shoulder with a foreleg, talons digging deep. When droplets of my blood stained the water, his tongue snaked out, capturing a few.

"She is Auril's daughter, true enough," another serpent said. "I checked in my own way, but her name is wrong."

"Could we debate this later?" I broke in. *"Mother's gone to rescue Titania and Ysir. They've apparently been imprisoned on Nemia."*

"We knew that part," the gray-black serpent said. "Auril stopped here and took a few of us with her to deal with the Unseelie sprites."

"She didn't bring enough," I told him. *"I was on my way to help, and she rerouted me here."*

"I will summon dragon aid," a red serpent said and shot toward the surface.

"We will accompany you," the serpent I'd begun thinking of as their leader told me. Before I could thank him, powerful magic shrouded me. The water, which had been quiet, rolled this way and that; everything went dark.

I haven't been in very many teleport spells not of my own making. Mother's and Cyn's had been the only ones.

The serpents' journey casting was so intense it would have sucked air from my lungs—if we hadn't been underwater and I'd still been breathing. I had to still be taking in oxygen, but the mechanism wasn't clear.

I kept expecting a transition point where we left water behind. There wasn't one. How many types of teleport enchantments were there, anyway?

Eh, my mind was tripping over itself on inconsequential details. I needed to be sharp. Goddess knew what we'd find when we arrived at Nemia. It couldn't be good, or Mother wouldn't have requested reinforcements. The serpents' magic prickled where it swirled around me, jabbing unpleasantly. Nothing but to ride it out. If they'd meant to harm me, I'd have sensed it.

The stabbing part didn't last long. Similar to my travel spells, the unremitting black began turning gray around the edges. The serpents had positioned me in the center of their group. Either to protect me or make certain I didn't get away. Maybe a smidgeon of both.

"Get ready." The gray-black serpent was back to mind speech.

I nodded, realized he was facing the wrong way to see me, and said, *"Got it."*

As quickly as it had taken shape, the serpents' casting shattered around us. It vibrated and then burst away leaving us in deep water, judging from its dark color. I took a moment to crane my neck back. If the ocean's surface was above us, it was so far away, I couldn't quite make it out. A lighter streak suggested daylight, but it could have been an optical illusion.

I blinked and switched to my psychic vision. A vast stone archway with suspended iron gates spread before us. Planted in the ocean floor, it was enormous. Vegetation and small crustaceans coated its surface until very little of the original stone remained visible. I assumed it was the entry to Nemia.

Where was Mother?

For that matter, where were the sprites we'd come to do battle with? And the other serpents? The serpents' leader swam forward. Burying his tail in the sand, he rose to an impressive height and began to chant in a language I'd never heard before.

Fish swam around us, but not as many as I'd have expected. Maybe we were too deep for decent feeding. Who had built this underwater city? Had it always been submerged? After a couple of minutes, the gates swung inward. If they made any noise, the weight of the water muffled it.

The serpents surged through, not waiting for the gates to fully open. I swam with them, but the gray-black one stopped me before I crossed beneath the archway. "I cannot protect you within," he said. "Not all who transit these gates return."

"I'll take my chances."

He looked at me squarely, taking my measure or assessing my magic. I must have met muster because he moved his bulk aside and I swam past him. Mother was inside, goddammit. If she'd bypassed her pride to ask for aid, it must be bad.

I'd no sooner cleared the gates when the serpent shot by me, and I heard a resounding thud that sounded like earth falling on a coffin. It was the gates slamming shut, but the sound held a finality that iced my bones.

Something about that thud changed everything. I was still underwater, but the surface was close. So close, I kicked my head back and broke through. An eerie beach spread before me. Stunted trees with black leaves reeked of poison. Behind them, the unmistakable sound of battle raged.

Did my magic even work here? No time like the present to get that little detail squared away. I called for a ward, and it obligingly shielded me. So far, so good. As prepared as I was likely to get, I sprinted for the squeaks and squeals coming from the tree line.

The serpents weren't as ungainly on land as I'd expected. Rows of tiny feet lined their bellies and propelled them forward. Similar to their dragon kin, they fought with fire. Everything in their path went up like a torch. To save time, I raised my mind voice and called for Mother.

She didn't answer.

I tried again. And again. I'd reached the trees. Fear gripped me, twisting my stomach into a hard painful knot. Mother had to be all right. She was immortal. The fallacy in my argument bit deep as I plunged into the fray, flattening horrible little creatures with stringy green hair and more teeth than they had any right to.

I'd fight until I found her, and then I'd fight some more. If these little fuckers had harmed Mother, I'd make certain none of them walked out of here. After that I'd turn my fury on the King of Winter. And maybe the Shadow Lords if they were a part of this.

Oberon made a huge mistake the day he'd chosen to fuck with me. I wouldn't rest until everything—and everyone—close to him lay in ruins.

✣ *9* ✣

CHAPTER NINE, CYN

We finished with the covenant in no time at all and sketched out the beginnings of a plan to tell Oberon his ploy failed, and he had to leave immediately. A delegation of unicorns would show up at Dubrova. If the Unseelie didn't yield—and produce Oberon—the unicorns would gore them.

My bet was the Unseelie would value their hides more than their allegiance to either Oberon or the Lord of Winter. The moment one of them fell, the others would hightail it out of there. Unseelie warriors are plenty brave, but also self-serving as hell. If there wasn't an immediate gain for them, they wouldn't stick around.

"We'll report in," the unicorns on the court told me.

"If there's any doubt," I said, "strike first."

"Oh, we will. Where will you be?" one asked.

"I'm going to Nemia to assist Auril and Dariyah," I replied, "but I'll travel with you to the castle." Once there, I'd check in with the serpents to see how many had gone with Auril and plan accordingly. Depending on their answer, I might rustle up some of our own warriors. Titania was their queen. They'd gladly fight for her.

When I reached the moat, I was warded to escape dealing with confrontations that might slow me down. I'd chafed at the delay back in the glade, but it had been too important not to see through to its end. I'd turned the newly ratified covenant and all its associated signature sheets over to the owls in Auril's realm. They'd promised to hide them well, and I couldn't very well bring them with me.

Nemia is a strange land. Its access is via the depths of Faery's one true ocean, but once you cross beneath its gates, the water part of things drops away. In times past, it served as the sea serpents' breeding ground, but they quit producing young around the time Oberon's insistence Faery was only for Fae intensified.

Not that they ever generated very many. One of the big downsides of immortality is too many progeny gums up the works since no one dies except in rare, unanticipated accidents.

Or wars.

The moat was empty. I made one more transit of it

to be certain. Indentations in the muddy bottom suggested serpents had been here recently. Had all of them left with Auril? It didn't bode well when the Queen of Air and Darkness, one of the most self-sufficient mages I'd ever known, requisitioned that level of aid.

A splash alerted me I wasn't alone in the water. It wasn't my preferred medium, so I kept my ward in place waiting to see who'd joined me. If it was one of the Unseelie bastards, I'd quietly teleport out of here. I couldn't afford wasting time on a project the unicorns had well in hand.

"Regent!"

I peered through the murky water, gave up, and switched to my third eye. A red sea serpent swam toward me at top speed. That she was still calling me Regent boded reasonably well. Not everyone had embraced Oberon's return. Hell, maybe no one did. We'd all been stoked when he'd finally left Faery.

"Where is everyone?" I asked her.

"First, Auril came. Some of us went with her. Then a Witch who wasn't one turned out to be Auril's daughter, and—" She stopped to blow a stream of bubbles through her mouth. "Anyway, she said Auril needed the rest of us. I called the dragons. They're on their way."

"Here or Nemia?"

"Where do you need them most, Regent?"

"Maybe a couple here to help the unicorns." Shielding my

telepathy, I told her our plans and asked if the rest of the dragons could join us in Nemia.

"I will let them know, Regent."

"Be careful," I called after her.

She flipped back around, graceful in her native element. *"None of us want Oberon back."*

I'd suspected as much and cobbled a teleport spell that would bring me out at Nemia's gates. If there was a way to teleport directly inside the land, I'd never found it. Precious moments slid past as I crossed to the ocean bottom and fumbled around remembering the incantation to urge the gates to open. They never remained that way, and this trip was no exception. I remembered the hollow clunk as they shut. It held a finality that had always unnerved me.

The crash and cries of battle hit me full on as soon as I was past the liminal space dividing Nemia from the rest of Faery. I covered the distance to the beach and sprinted for the trees, taking care to avoid touching them. I'd never understood why the entry was ringed with poisonous shrubbery, but Nemia had been one of Faery's first worlds. Separate, yet connected, it reminded me of Fire Mountain in that regard.

Nothing about the rest of it was anything like the dragons' arid world.

A herd of Unseelie sprites yowled as they bore down on me. They smelled like roadkill, but some things never changed. Focusing a beam of destruction to laser precision, I sliced two of them in half. Entrails spilled on the ground; Nemia made short work of them. I'd forgotten that part about this world. It absorbed anything with blood.

The other eight sprites kept on coming. Not overly bright, they stood maybe four feet tall. Stringy green hair grew in clumps from their otherwise bald scalps. Teeth sprouted from their oversized mouths, visible when their jaws flapped open. Some had two eyes, some only one. It had been centuries since I'd seen one. Through the lens of modern science, they looked like someone's genetic experiment gone bad.

I killed two more. The other six backed off, giving me a wide berth. Hmmm. Maybe not as stupid as they used to be. The Unseelie must have commandeered them as cannon fodder since they kept marching forward no matter what happened to the ones in front of them.

Did it mean no one was leading the charge?

Seemed impossible. An Unseelie warrior or two had to be somewhere because the sprites couldn't have masterminded abducting Titania and Ysir and hauling them here.

I scanned the woods ahead. The only poison trees were those guarding the entrance to Nemia. The rest of the vegetation didn't burn like acid if you brushed up against it. Serpents battled sprites in brawling clumps. Every direction was filled with conflict as far as I could see. The moat must have housed fifty serpents; all of them were here save the female I'd spoken with.

I sent a slender beam of seeking magic to find Dariyah. She was maybe a kilometer from me. I ran toward her, augmenting my pace with magic. While I ran, I hunted for Titania and Ysir and Auril. Auril was with Dariyah, but I couldn't find the other two. They must be well warded.

Or buried so deep my magic couldn't penetrate the walls around them.

I shelved that last thought. One problem at a time. I'd discarded my ward in the interest of expediency. Not the swiftest move. I shot into a grove of hawthorn trees and skidded to a halt.

Dariyah was on her knees with Auril in her arms. Her lips were skinned back from her teeth; power arced around her and her mother in a protective shelter. The Unseelie warriors I'd been certain had to be here had formed a circle around the two women.

I counted six as they glanced my way out of their odd, pale eyes, some silver, some gray, some white. The Unseelie possess an otherworldly beauty that outshines anything Fae and the remainder of the Seelie court as well. With their bare chests painted with runes in silver and gold, the batch ringed around Auril and Dariyah could have walked into any Hollywood studio and been snapped up whether they could act or not. Their beauty was pervasive, striking. Once a mortal laid eyes on an Unseelie, they spent the rest of their days in mourning, certain they'd never see anything as perfect again.

I wrenched my attention away from my dark-hearted kinsfolk. If Dariyah was aware of my presence, she hadn't given any indication. Auril's eyes were closed, her breathing labored. I leapt over the Unseelie and landed squarely next to the women.

"What happened?" I growled.

"They did something to her," Dariyah ground out. "Happened before I got here."

"Have you seen Titania or Ysir?"

Dariyah shook her head. She was funneling power into her mother, but some was slopping over, and Nemia sucked it up. Must be a nice change from blood and guts.

"Looks like this is our lucky day." One of the Unseelie grinned, displaying a mouthful of very white, very even teeth. His gray eyes glowed with anticipation.

I knew him. Actually, I had a passing acquaintance with them all from the days when they'd lived in Faery with the rest of us. I grinned back. "Don't count those hens yet."

He shrugged. "Three of you. Two-and-a-half since

Auril's not exactly in the game. Six of us. Not much of a contest."

"Maybe not. I beat you at dice, though. Cards too. And bested you in a jousting tournament."

"Only because you cheated. My unicorn threw me."

"You treated him like a horse. Besides, no one rides unicorns. You were a fool to try." Memories of that event surfaced, clear as if they'd happened yesterday.

The Unseelie laughed. "They are horses. With horns. If you Fae hadn't given them the kid-glove treatment, they'd know their place."

So long as he was in a talkative mood, I asked, "What'd you do to Auril?"

"King's orders." He turned his hands palms up. "I'm just the help around here."

"Which king?" Dariyah gritted.

"Why the only one who matters." The Unseelie ogled her in a way I didn't like at all. "The King of Winter."

"I figured Oberon was a puppet," I tossed out.

"Aye, well you always were smarter than him," another Unseelie said. "Good thing for us he hates you and doesn't listen to your counsel."

Insight dawned. "You set it up like that. Maybe not you personally, but the King of Winter."

"Bingo. Cynwrigg is up two," the first Unseelie chortled.

"What did the King of Winter order you to do to Auril?" I pressed. He'd been right about my odds being crappy, but sooner or later the serpents or dragons would find their way to us.

"Use your imagination, Fae," the Unseelie sneered. "She was his. She walked away. No one does that to the King of Winter."

"Maybe she didn't quite see it that way." Dariyah gripped Auril tighter as if she were worried her mother might sink so deep no one could reach her.

"Upstart bitch. He'll pound sense into her," the second Unseelie said.

"Speaking of which," the first one chimed in. "Time for us to go. We have what we came for, and—"

Dariyah snarled. "Over my dead body." The power sheeting from her developed reddish overtones.

"It may come to that," the Unseelie said pleasantly. "But it would be such a shame. Such a waste of glorious womanhood."

"Back off. She's mine," I told him.

He turned a startled glance my way. "What do you mean yours? No one in Faery mates for life. Tell you what. We could share her. I'm good with that."

"I'm not." I positioned myself as best I could. My back was still my weak point with two Unseelie behind me, so I turned one hundred eighty degrees and faced outward. At least that way between Dariyah and me we could see all of our adversaries.

"I can't let go of her," she whispered into my mind.

"Open your magic to me. I've got this."

"We can hear you," an Unseelie taunted.

"Aye, cobble all the magic in your puny stable together," the first one urged. "The outcome will be the same. Just give us Auril. We'll leave. No one loses a wink of sleep over the bitch. I'll even renounce my claim on your 'mate' since you're not willing to share her."

I could have pointed out he'd never had a claim, but it wasn't worth wasting words. Why hadn't anyone stumbled across us? We weren't that far away from the bulk of the fighting. It didn't matter they heard me when I called for Titania and Ysir. And the serpents. I left dragons out of the equation. If they showed up, they'd be my little surprise.

"Titania is here?" the first Unseelie raised his white brows. His surprise was genuine and proved he had, indeed, intercepted my telepathic request for assistance.

"You pegged it," another said. "This truly is our lucky day. We'll get both sisters—nay, both queens—for the trouble of one."

"You'll have to locate her first," I said, ladling lots of sugar into my words. "I've been trying since I arrived."

"Ysir is the librarian, right?" the Unseelie didn't miss a beat.

"The same," I said.

"He's dangerous," another Unseelie noted. "Way more powerful than he ever lets on."

Not how I would have described him, but good to know, nonetheless.

Half a dozen sea serpents slithered into the clearing and formed their own circle around the Unseelie. "Sorry, Regent," one hissed. "Illusion shields your presence in this spot."

"We have to get Auril to a healer," Dariyah said. "She's fading beyond my reach." Anguish scoured her words.

No more reason to run out the clock. Reinforcements were here. Staunch bugling told me dragons had arrived. Alarm twisted six Unseelie faces into expressions that made them less lovely than they'd been a moment before. An immense golden dragon circled to land, followed by a blue and a green. Fire streamed from their mouths, setting one of the Unseelie on fire.

It wouldn't kill him, but it had to hurt. Magefire is like ignited gasoline, burning with a mind and purpose of its own.

The Unseelie rolled on the ground, but the fire burned on. He left the grove, running flat out for the ocean. It wouldn't put the flames out, either, but I didn't bother to rain on his parade. He'd find out soon enough.

Meanwhile, the serpents had begun shooting their

own fire willy-nilly. Sometimes it connected, sometimes not. They were playing with the Unseelie, and the Unseelie recognized the ploy.

"What will it be?" the gold dragon bugled. "If you leave now, we won't chase you down and annihilate you."

"Will you withdraw the fire burning our kinsman?" the Unseelie who'd been doing most of the talking asked.

"We'll consider it. Once you're well and truly gone. We'll know." The dragon folded his forelegs across his broad chest.

"This is above my paygrade," the Unseelie announced to the others. "It was supposed to be easy in, easy out. I didn't sign us up for a battle."

"Our king isn't going to see it that way," another muttered.

"Fuck him. We won't go back to Faery," the first one said.

I grinned. "Looks like I might be the lucky one," I called after their retreating forms, and then focused my attention on Dariyah. Tears were falling, forming a small fortune in gems around her mother's prostrate form.

The golden dragon squatted and held out his forelegs. "Give her to me. I will bring her to our healers."

"I'm not leaving Mother." Dariyah met his whirling gaze. Gutsy of her.

"Fine. Get on. I'll bring both of you to Fire Mountain."

Before it fully registered what was happening, Dariyah had handed Auril to the dragon and vaulted onto his back. I knew her well enough to recognize how worried she must be, but her face was lined with determination.

"I'll meet you there," I yelled just before all the dragons vanished. The backwash from their teleport magic drove me to my knees. Apparently, they didn't require Nemia's gateway to exit the land.

I wanted to follow her, but I had to find Titania. If the Unseelie king hadn't nabbed her and Ysir, it meant they'd come to this spot under their own power and were hiding. Presumably from Oberon.

"Help me locate the queen," I told the serpents.

"We've been looking, but to no avail. The sprites are either dead or they left," one told me.

"Strong work," I said, adding, "and above and beyond. You shall receive commendations for your efforts this day. Fan out and hunt for Titania and Ysir with me."

Nemia isn't all that large. Magic flared, sending sparklers that turned the air iridescent as all of us searched. Usually, someone would have come up with clues, a scent track or something, but when we came back together on the beach we had nothing.

"Are you certain they're here?" a serpent asked me.

"Faery seemed to think they were," I told him.

"That was quite a while ago," another serpent pointed out. "They could have switched locations."

"Aye, it's what I'd have done if I was concerned about discovery," the first serpent said.

We weren't doing any good milling about here. We could do ten more passes and come up empty-handed. "Return to Faery," I told them.

"Where will you be, Regent?" one asked.

I set my mouth in a grim line. "I'll do one more sweep here, and then I'm going to Fire Mountain to make certain Auril is all right."

One by one, the serpents glided into the water. They'd find the gate, pass through it, and teleport from there. Sinking to my knees, I splayed my hands on the sand and sent power auguring through Nemia. If Titania or Ysir were still here, I'd know it.

We're all made of the same stuff, we Fae. Our power resonates at a particular frequency, and all of us are sensitive to it. Convinced they'd left, I wrapped myself in magic and dove into the water. The gates rose before me, opening without any intervention from me.

It brought a wry smile to my face. Nemia was sick of conflict. While the land may have welcomed Titania and the Fae librarian, that welcome had been short-lived.

"Thank you for your forbearance," I said as I passed

beneath the gate and set a journey spell for Fire Mountain. Once I'd known the King of Winter reasonably well. He liked to toy with his victims, which suggested Auril had only been sunk in spells.

Dariyah wouldn't have worn such a lost, haunted look if things weren't serious, though.

Maybe the King of Winter had grown sloppy in his older years. Or more bloodthirsty. He'd had centuries to plot revenge against his wandering consort. He might not care what happened to her, how much pain she suffered, so long as she was brought to heel.

I urged my spell to greater speed, worried if I didn't get there soon, it might be too late. The dragons were talented mages, but their power was keyed to their own kind.

Should we have brought Auril to Faery instead of Fire Mountain?

Eh, that wouldn't have worked, either. Too close to Oberon and the King of Winter. Concern carved a trail through me as my spell carried me forward. I'd find out soon enough how much damage they'd done, and then I'd set a course to mitigate the worst of it.

❦ 10 ❦

CHAPTER TEN, DARIYAH

I was riding a dragon. A genuine, fire-breathing dragon. I should be filled with wonder, taking mental notes to make certain I didn't miss a second of the flight. Instead, I was too worried about Mother to do anything but funnel magic into her and pray to every goddess who'd ever walked to not let her drop into oblivion.

Holding her in my arms, feeling her life force ebbing, had rattled me more than anything I'd ever dealt with. Mother was strong, invincible. Nothing could get the better of her.

Except, apparently, her erstwhile consort.

Why had she never told me about him? Was she ashamed?

Was he my father?

Nah, impossible. Neither Fae nor Sidhe shed jewels when they cried. I figured whoever my father was, he'd been a total fucktard bastard, but thank the gods it hadn't been the King of Winter.

Heat from the beast beneath me seared my legs through my trousers. Sweat dripped down my face and flanks. The scales had sharp edges too. Not that I'd make a habit of riding dragons, but if it ever happened again, I needed thick leather pants. We soared through blackness; the only reason I could see anything was because the dragon glowed a whitish-gold.

My magic was tangled with Mother's. At least she wasn't any worse. I sensed the dragon's enchantment too, also firmly intwined with the core of Mother's power. The dragon's magic was vast with fire as the leading element. My strong suit has always been earth with air a close second. I'd never thought to ask which element was primary for Fae.

Perhaps that would be a way to narrow my parentage down.

You've already done that, my inner voice noted dryly. *He's a dragon or a unicorn.*

For once I answered back. *Maybe something else cries precious tears.*

Yeah? Like what?

I lacked an answer. Chalk it up to my slipshod magical education. Plus, Mother would have dodged sharing information that might have helped me figure out who the other half of my gene pool had been.

I slapped my forehead with a palm. I'd been so frantic about Mother, manners had deserted me. "Thank you so much for your aid," I told the golden dragon.

My words were yanked into the slipstream, and I started to repeat them in telepathy, when he said, "Your need was great."

"She's not any worse," I ventured.

"Not my assessment. I'm moving as quickly as I can. Fire Mountain is much farther away than Faery's other worlds."

His words were like a punch to the guts. A bitter taste filled my mouth, and I tasted bile. His magic was infinitely more powerful than mine. He'd sensed something I'd missed. My anxiety shot through the roof.

"She can't die," I mumbled.

"Some fates are worse than death," the dragon rumbled. Smoke and steam puffed through his open jaws.

Questions tumbled round and round in my mind. I didn't ask any of them because I'm a coward. I didn't want to know. So long as I was ignorant, nothing bad would happen to Mother.

For fuck's sake. I'm not twelve anymore, I rebuked myself.

"How much longer to Fire Mountain?"

"It takes as long as it takes," he said.

Eh, for all I knew, my mount could be female. I'd made assumptions because of its size. "You probably already know, but my name is Dariyah," I murmured, hoping the dragon would share its name in response.

"It may be the name you use, but it is not yours," the dragon said firmly.

"Do you know my true name?" I asked.

"Aye." The dragon stopped there.

"But you're not going to tell me," I pressed.

"'Tisn't mine to share," he replied.

"Mmph. I suppose you know who my father was too."

"Aye."

This time I didn't bother to ask for clarification. No point. If he was going to tell me, he already would have. I zeroed in on Mother and let out a tense breath. She didn't seem any worse to me, but neither was she better. The dragon had intimated she was in grave danger.

Disgusted with myself, I strapped on a set and asked, "Do you know what's wrong with Mother?"

A lengthy silence ensued, long enough I began to think this was another question he'd dodge. I couldn't make him talk with me. He'd been more than generous bringing me with him. Or perhaps it hadn't been generosity at all, but expediency. He'd sensed—and rightly—I'd have argued about being parted from Mother.

"Did you know about her alliance with the King of Winter?" The dragon's question came out of left field.

"No. It happened a long time before I was born."

"I intuited as much"—the dragon's tone was a rebuke—"but she might have told you of her history in Faery."

"She did, but it appears she omitted key elements."

"I see."

I felt a shift characteristic of all teleport spells and understood we were close to our destination. "Is there anything I need to know before we arrive?" I asked.

"Remain quiet and as out of sight as possible. We do not welcome visitors."

Alarm sluiced through me. "I can remain by Mother's side, though. Right?"

"Maybe. It depends on the healer who takes over her care."

"You never did tell me what's wrong with her." I winced. My tone hadn't been particularly gracious. More surly and demanding than anything else.

"I am not certain, but her essence keeps trying to escape from her body, as if it's seeking a home elsewhere."

"Essence as in magic?"

"Nay, child. Essence as in soul. The part of her that will continue regardless of her circumstances."

I didn't understand. Why would she run? Why now when she'd just been reunited with me? With her sister and her native soil. Was the specter of dealing with the King of Winter as horrid as all that?

Or was it unwillingness to face a mistake that had finally circled back and bitten her in the ass? Mother had a stiff-necked aspect. Even more than most, she didn't like to make mistakes. Owning up to them had never been an element in her wheelhouse.

Of course, I hadn't understood that until I was well and truly gone from the remote spot I'd grown up. Kicking myself for thinking even a single negative thought about Mother, I visualized her getting past this. I'd give her all the assistance I could.

It still hadn't quite registered my *persona non grata* status in Faery had lifted, but it wouldn't make much difference if we couldn't oust Oberon.

Got to believe, I lectured myself as the dragon's spell blasted outward.

Heat bore down on me like a live thing. The few droplets of sweat from the dragon's hide turned into a veritable flood, and my clothing soaked through immediately. Two relentless suns sat overhead. Beneath us, rocks and sand spread in every direction. In the distance, volcanoes belched smoke and fire.

Just like the dragons. No wonder they adore it here.

The dragon slewed left and brought us down in a spot that looked like every other place in this barren world. I was panting because breathing fried the inside of my nose and lungs. I tucked my nose into the crook of an elbow. It helped a little.

The dragon had said they didn't get many visitors. My bet was not many non-dragons would volunteer to spend much time here. Two dragons hurried forward, surprisingly agile for all their bulk. One was almost white, the other black.

"This is my patient?" the white one asked.

Interesting. The dragon who'd brought us here had clearly called ahead, but I hadn't been privy to his telepathy. One more example of how badly my power measured up. I was used to pitting myself against anything magical and coming out the winner.

Not here.

"Aye, Elana." The gold dragon transferred Mother into the other dragon's forelegs.

He'd told me to keep a low profile, but I'd be damned if I'd sit still while the healer dragon waltzed off with Mother. How would I be able to find her? I was fairly certain my tracking skills wouldn't work on this world. I dropped my arm from in front of my nose and mouth and jumped to the ground twisting a bit of magic into a canopy to break my fall.

My first lungful of air minus my arm stung like a bitch. Sweat sheeted into my eyes, and I was panting. "Wait," I cried.

The white dragon turned back around. "Who are you? Och. Don't bother to tell me. No time."

"Her daughter. I'm her daughter," I croaked. Sheesh. The overheated air was frying my vocal cords along with everything else.

Magic scoured me from my head to my feet. The dragon's eyes might have widened, but they spun so fast, it was hard to tell. "You cannot come with me," she said.

"I will take her into the caves," the dragon who'd brought me said.

"But where will Mother be?" I started forward, but tripped and sprawled on the hot sandy soil. My feet had been on fire; even stout boot soles were no protection from the dirt. When my entire body contacted the ground, I muffled a shriek.

"Get up," the gold dragon bugled. It wasn't a suggestion.

I'd have scrambled upright, anyway. Remaining where I was was a non-starter. Suicide by bake oven. By the time I got my feet under me, the other two dragons were gone.

"Walk forward," the gold dragon said.

A band of cliffs sat dead ahead, but I didn't argue. The closer we got to the rocks, the hotter it grew. And then there were no more cliffs, and we were inside a dimly lit rounded enclosure. At least we were out from under those harsh suns.

Breath whooshed from me in raspy pants. "Where is Mother?"

"Safe." He lumbered around in front of me and glared. "I specifically told you to keep your mouth shut. What part of that escaped you?"

It was probably a combination of the heat and my sweat-soaked hair dripping down my forehead and panic Mother was going to die in this alien world all by herself, but something snapped. It had been a long while since I'd taken orders from anyone, and I didn't aim to start now.

Straightening my back, I stood as tall as I could. It didn't rival the dragon's eight-foot height at the top of his shoulders, let along his curved neck, but he'd respect me, goddammit.

"None of it 'escaped me,'" I mimicked his tone. "But I don't take orders from you."

"Here, you do," he said. "Or you shall leave. I allowed your presence because your kinswoman is gravely injured."

"What good is my presence if I'm not with her?" I ground out.

His eerie eyes spun faster, reminding me of out-of-control pinwheels. "No one outside of our kind has ever witnessed dragon healing. We are not about to begin with you."

"But what harm could I do?" It was past time to shut up, but desperation drove me.

"Lots," he said succinctly. "For starters, you could insert your power at an inopportune time and completely destroy your mother's chances of survival. They weren't good when she arrived."

I opened my mouth to protest I'd never do that, but shut it again. If I believed Mother was in danger from some dragon ministration or other, I sure as hell would step in.

"See?" The dragon raised a scaled brow.

Great. Not a thought to call my own. I swiped my forearm across my forehead. At least the flood of sweat had slowed. It wasn't exactly cool where we were, but the dark warmth was welcome in contrast to the blazing suns.

"What's your name?" I asked pointblank. Offering him (her?) mine hadn't bought me much.

"Names hold power. Yours doesn't because it isn't your real one, but—"

"Fine," I broke in. "What should I call you?"

"Ash will do."

It pinged sourly off my magic. Crap. Why was I so sensitive to everyone else's faux names but not to my own?

Ash trudged out of the entry cave. He hadn't told me to follow him, but I did. A generous corridor wound downward. The lower we got, the cooler it became until we reached a level that was almost temperate. The sound of water running over rocks had been teasing me for a while. After about six twists and turns in the passageway, an underground river came into view.

I started for the water, but common sense kicked me in the ass. "May I drink?" I asked. For all I knew, it was spiked with something that was nectar to dragons but deadly to those like me.

Whatever the hell I was.

"Aye. It is why I brought you here."

Before I fell face down in the creek, I asked, "Any word about Mother?"

"Not yet."

Was he telling me the truth? How could I ever figure it out? His mind was closed to me. Clawing my way inside would never work. He'd up the ante on his warding system. Kneeling by the water, I cupped some in my hands and rinsed my overheated face. Next, I drank deep. It had a sweetish taste, one I've always associated with minerals. Made sense. We were deep underground.

I settled on a flat rock. Time slid past. I had no idea how much. I've never bothered with a timepiece. My connection with the natural world has been more than sufficient to give me a rough approximation of what time it is. But I wasn't connected to anything here. I've never felt so much like an outsider, like I was treading on hallowed ground and doing my damnedest not to leave any footprints.

When I caught a snoutful of whiskey and wildflowers, I thought I was hallucinating, that I'd been underground so long my senses were playing tricks on me. Lifting my head, my nostrils flared. There it was again, but stronger now. I hadn't imagined Cyn's signature scent. Bolting upright, I called, "Cynwrigg?"

My timing was good because he emerged from the bend in the corridor hiding the creek from view. "Dariyah. Thanks be to the goddess." He turned and bowed to the gold dragon. "Many thanks to you as well for keeping her safe."

"Glad to do it, Regent," he rumbled amidst smoky plumes of flame.

"That's scarcely true," I spoke up. "It's not like I've been a model guest."

The dragon snorted smoke and laughter. "I've seen worse."

"How's Auril?" Cyn broke in.

"I don't know." Trotting to his side, I walked into his arms, craving their comfort and the solidly familiar feel of him against me.

The dragon's head snapped up. "Elana approaches," he said about the same time the white dragon walked toward us with Mother in her arms. Magic surged from me as I sought evidence she was alive.

"It's all right," Cyn murmured. "She's still with us."

"You must return her to Faery," Elana said. "To her court. I have done all I can, but it may not be enough."

"What was wrong?" I asked.

"Many things," the dragon replied. "I've stabilized what I could, but she must want to recover. That element is beyond my control."

"Dying is easy," Cyn muttered.

I knew the second half of that saying. "Yeah, it's living that takes guts and imagination." I held out my arms for Mother.

"I'll take her," Cynwrigg said.

"Can we teleport from down here? Or do we need to be outside?" I asked.

"I will see you home from this spot," the gold dragon said.

"Take us to the Midnight Court, please." Cyn nodded his way.

Considering how long it had taken to travel from Nemia to Fire Mountain, I was shocked when the hidden glade beneath Faery formed around us in a matter of moments. Our guide didn't remain long enough for me to thank him.

Cyn arranged Mother on her back on a grassy knoll in the midst of a grove of ancient trees. I sat at her head and placed it in my lap, gratified by the gentle rise and fall of her chest. Animals streamed out of the forest, arranging themselves around her.

"Did you find Titania and Ysir?" I asked.

"Nay. They might have been on Nemia, but I found no trace of either their presence or their passing."

With my hands on either side of Mother's head, I probed for anything that might help bring her back. The pitched battle to keep life within her wasn't a problem any longer. Whatever Elana had done had brought her some measure of peace, but not enough to encourage her to open her eyes.

I met Cyn's direct gaze. "What in the fuck did the Winter King do to her? Why did she leave him?"

"Tried to force his will on her. I don't have all the bits and pieces, but there were children she refused to bear. She sent their souls back to the place they reside between lives. He locked her into various prisons; she escaped them all. Finally, one day she told him she was done and walked out.

"Next we heard, she'd formed the Midnight Court. All were welcome there save the King of Winter. Even Oberon would have been accepted if he'd chosen to visit, but he never did."

I smoothed hair exactly like mine back from Mother's forehead. "Come back to me," I whispered. When I looked up, hordes of animals had arrived, standing ringed around Mother. From fawns and deer and wolves and bears to smaller creatures. Birds winged overhead singing and cawing.

The earth broke apart between two thick tree boles. Titania crawled out with Ysir behind her. "Told you this would work," he crowed and then glanced around out of his rheumy eyes. "Oh my goodness, just look at all of them."

"No one likes a know-it-all," Titania retorted sharply and made a beeline for her sister. Before I could react, she squatted next to Auril and slapped her face. "You do not get to check out, Sister. Just because the going got tough and that asshole showed back up."

"You. Will. Not. Do. That. Again," I growled.

"I'll do whatever I damn well please, girlie." She tossed her head. "I'm your aunt, and you'd do well to remember it."

"Auril." Titania gripped one of her hands and squeezed hard enough I heard bones cracking together.

I sent a jolt of magic at Titania's hand. She didn't even flinch. Sheesh. Was my power not a match for anyone's?

Mother writhed under my hands. Her eyes fluttered open and settled on Titania's face. "All right. All right. You've made your point. Let go of my hand."

Titania's lined face split into a warm smile. "That's more like it. You never were a quitter."

"I was taking a break."

"Aye, well, you don't get to do that, either."

I felt like I'd joined a very old conversation, one that had its roots long before I came along. Ysir was wandering among the animals, petting and cooing. An owl perched on one of his shoulders; a raven had taken up residence on the other.

Mother struggled to a sit. I got to my feet and walked to Cynwrigg. A corner of his mouth turned down. "Nothing like a bit of sisterly love to bring things around, eh?"

"I wouldn't know," I said stiffly. I'd always longed for siblings, but they'd have had downsides too.

I'd die before admitting it, but I was hurt she hadn't spared a single glance my way. Eh, I'd get over myself. I turned to Cyn and said, "How about dinner at Lady Luck?"

"We can't be gone long," he cautioned, "but food will be thin here since Dubrova is barred to us, and the land is under siege." He beckoned to Ysir. "Where were you?"

The old librarian tottered over to us. "Traveling, Regent. You told me to keep our queen safe. I'd say I did a most excellent job."

"I'd say the same," Cyn agreed. "Are you hungry?"

"We found food a plenty on our travels, Titania and me. Even brought some provisions back with us."

Cyn patted his shoulder, careful not to dislodge the

bird. "Excellent. See that Auril eats something. We'll be back in an hour or so, and then we'll figure out what our next moves are."

"Getting that usurper out of Dubrova." Ysir sounded outraged. "What other task could there possibly be. I want my library back. My home. My—"

"We'll attempt to do all of that," Cynwrigg reassured him.

"Thank you, Regent, I am certain you shall." Ysir ambled back into the pack of wildlife, and I crafted a spell to take us to Earth. Maybe if I left, Mother would notice I was gone.

Maybe not.

She and Titania were chatting up a storm, heads bent together.

"Sisters and daughters are different," Cynwrigg said softly. "Come on. You'll feel better with a hot meal and a couple of glasses of spirits in you."

I loosed my spell, humiliated he'd been inside my pity-party of a mind. Sometimes the best words are no words, so I didn't talk at all on our brief junket to the stairs leading upward into Lady Luck.

CHAPTER ELEVEN, CYN

"How are you doing?" I asked Dariyah. I kept the question neutral, offering her infinite choices of what to address when she answered me. She'd been quiet since we left Faery. I didn't blame her. Auril might have been through a lot, but ignoring her daughter didn't cut it. Not in my book.

Dariyah looked up from the meal spread on the small table in my office and shrugged. "Better. I'm glad Mother came around." Her mouth twisted wryly. "She seems to be the only one who can tell me what my name is or who my father was. If she checks out, I'll never know."

I could have said many things, but this wasn't a time for me to underwrite the insidious lies we tell ourselves for so long they turn into truth. "Those aren't the only reasons you're relieved she'll be all right. You love her."

"Guilty as charged, but it's worse than that." Dariyah narrowed her gaze and stared into my eyes.

"What do you mean?"

"She is the only creature I've ever loved. The only person. I'm not counting animals that have passed through my life. I've loved them to pieces, but it's different."

She'd kicked the door open, so I stuck my foot out to hold it there. "No husbands? No girlfriends? No partners?"

Dariyah shook her head from side to side. "None of the above. I've been a regular one-woman band." Her intense gaze shaded to defensiveness. "Does it matter?"

"Not at all."

I shielded my thoughts, but I must have been a touch too late because she said, "I do not want your pity."

Reaching across the table, I caught one of her hands and held on even after she tried to tug it out from under me. After jettisoning my warding, I said, "It isn't pity. Look deeper. You've had a difficult life, and I'm partly responsible for it."

"How?" She managed to yank her hand away and buried it in her lap with the other one.

"I stood by while Faery hung onto antiquated laws. I

understood they were wrong, but I didn't do anything to fix them." Taking a measured breath, I went on. "I never wanted to be Faery's regent. Mostly, I saw myself as a placeholder because I expected Oberon to return. After maybe forty years, it dawned on me I had to up my game, but it still took another twenty or thirty before I got serious about dealing with the rift and looking beyond my own needs."

"That's when you ended up here, huh?" She gazed around my cramped office on the casino's fourth floor.

"Yeah."

"We have to get rid of him. And that Winter King person too." A fierce undertone emphasized her words. Her face hardened, turning her beauty into something untamed.

"We do," I agreed, "but talk is cheap. Whatever we do must be permanent. I do not plan to fight the same war again and again."

"Say more," she urged.

My thoughts weren't much more than half baked, but I forged ahead anyway. "The King of Winter will be the simpler of the two."

"Why? His minions weren't scrounged from the *Dreaming*. They appear to actually work for him."

"Because he doesn't have a stake in Faery. His only claim was through Auril with her link to Titania. When she left, his days were numbered unless he shaped up.

He'd broken rule after rule sending his Unseelie disciples among mortals to wreak destruction."

Dariyah drew her red brows together. "What? So he got a buy because of Mother? I thought Fae and Sidhe and all other brands of mages were welcome in Faery."

"That last part is true," I replied. "But in his case, he was extended latitude we'd never have offered anyone else, and all on account of Auril. The court censured his actions so many times it turned into a standing joke. He'd look contrite, promise he'd leave his wicked ways behind, and then in a month or a year, there we'd be all over again."

"Oberon did nothing, huh?"

"Nope, and now I'm thinking the two of them were in cahoots even then. Except the King of Winter could run magical rings around Oberon."

"Ha! Bet that's not how Oberon saw things," she sneered. "The little I've seen of him, he's one arrogant son of a bitch."

"You've pegged him right," I said. "Which is interesting because I've spent the last several centuries making excuses for every one of his failings."

She pushed out of her chair and came around to my side of the table. I moved my chair back and patted my lap. When she perched on it, I threaded my arms around her waist. After a slight hesitation, she hugged me too.

"We can't go back," she said. "No matter how much we'd like to."

"I can't afford to make any more mistakes, either," I pointed out. "My slipshod leadership is why we're where we are today."

"Pfft. No one has that much power. Not even you." After nuzzling my neck, she went back to the remains of her meal and dug into it.

We needed to finish eating and hustle back to Faery, so I polished what was left on my plate too. When she set down her fork, she said, "Oberon had a heavy-handed way about him. Makes sense you'd do the opposite. It's kind of like raising kids. None of us like how we were raised, so we do something different with our own. Sometimes it works out. Sometimes it doesn't."

"And how would you know about such things?" I teased.

She smiled. "I don't. Not directly. But I've given at least a thought or two to how I'd raise children of my own."

"Not on a distant world would be my first guess."

She snorted. "Oh, you mean without friends to play with, gal pals to trade secrets with, and anyone besides the two of us? You'd be right about that, but I realize my case was extreme." Dariyah angled her head to one side, forehead creased in thought.

I left my seat, walked around the table, and drew her to her feet. "What are you thinking?"

She closed her teeth over her lower lip and then said, "I lack evidence, but I've always felt Mother was grooming me for something, that she had plans for me that ran well beyond my growing-up years. Leaving was my idea, not hers, but I couldn't tolerate the thought of staying where I was forever. She warned me if I left I'd never see her again, but with all her scrying she must have known it wasn't true."

"You're seeing it more as a ploy to keep you there?"

"Maybe. Yeah. What else could it have been?"

"Have you ever asked her about it?" I beckoned to Dariyah and we walked out of my office, heading for the stairs that would spit us out in Faery.

"For what? You've seen how she is. Information is doled out on a need-to-know basis."

We dropped below the casino's basement level. "Things might be different now," I said thoughtfully.

"In what way?"

"Surely Auril is aware how close she came to fading from every world. If that had happened, who would tell you about her plans?"

Dariyah stopped at the bottom of a flight of stairs close enough to Faery's boundary I felt its pull and turned to face me. "Whatever this is isn't all that simple. She might be ashamed—or guilty. She went to great lengths to birth me and rear me, to ensure my survival. If whatever she's seen in her pool—or her glass or rattling bones—casts me into a role I have no interest in, she's waiting."

"For what?"

"Not sure." Dariyah shrugged. "Maybe to box me into a corner where I have no choice but to capitulate."

"Hush." I draped my arms around her and held her against me, reveling in the feel of her body in my arms. The heat of her, the silk of her skin. "Whatever this is—and it may be nothing—you're not alone anymore. I won't stand by and let Auril or anyone else manipulate you for their ends."

She splayed her hands across my back and tucked her head into the hollow between my neck and shoulders. "But you barely know me."

"What I know"—I tipped her chin until her eyes met mine—"is our magic was destined to be joined. And us with it. I've never put much stock in divination, neither have I chased prophecies with me in the center of them, but I bet if I did, I'd find you."

"A regular Catherine and Heathcliff?"

"Not star-crossed lovers," I corrected her. "Star-destined ones."

She rose onto her toes and brushed her lips across mine. Weaving my hands into her hair, I kissed her back breathing in the fresh, wild scent of her and wishing I could stop time right here. Hold us in this spot until we'd drunk our fill of one another. It could take centuries, millennia.

She swiped her tongue across my mouth and murmured, "You have the soul of a bard. No wonder you never warmed to being Faery's regent."

I twisted a lock of her hair around my finger. "Bards faded with the passing of time."

"Aye, but we didn't." She'd switched to Gaelic, the syllables soft and melodic against my ears.

With my arms still around her, I conjured the magic to bring us out in the glade marking the Midnight Court. When we'd left, it had been full to overflowing with birds and animals. Now, it stretched empty before us. Where had everyone gone? With a great deal of reluctance, I let go of Dariyah and sent my magic ranging free in hopes of locating somebody who knew something.

"I felt that." Ysir tottered toward us from the direction of a lush grove of evergreens. The raven and owl still rode on his shoulders. My guess was they were the same birds from earlier.

"Where are Titania and Auril?" I asked.

"They bade me wait for you. They've retired to Auril's home, setting it to rights after it being empty for so long." His gaze turned skyward, and he pointed.

"Finally, nightfall is nearly upon us. My but I'd grown weary of perpetual daylight."

"Might be a good sign," Dariyah murmured.

"How so, Witch?" Ysir cast a sidelong glance Dariyah's way.

She smiled at the wizened librarian. "It must mean Oberon couldn't force Faery to his will like he did before. Wasn't the 'no night' structure his doing?"

"You might have a point." Ysir bobbed his head.

"Has anyone visited Faery since our return?" I asked.

"When would we have had time?" Ysir flapped his hands and made a sour face. "You'd think time wouldn't be a problem since we live forever. But it is. Never enough of the stuff."

How were the unicorns doing with their assignment? If I reached out with telepathy, would I put them in danger? It's impossible to totally shield mind speech from those who want to listen in.

"I'm going to Dubrova," I said. "The unicorns were supposed to present their proposal. Seems like I should have heard from them by now, but I haven't. Oberon must not have been in a bargaining mood."

"I'll go with you." Dariyah stood straighter.

I'd assumed she'd find Auril and Titania. Her quick offer of support warmed me. She'd said the only person she'd ever loved was her mother, but perhaps I was inveigling my way past the walls she'd erected and cultivated to keep people out.

"Auril said I was to bring you to her." Ysir tried to stand taller, but the cracks and pops in his spine must have hurt.

Dariyah frowned. "Did she say why?"

"Nay. She did not."

"All right. No need to make a special trip, but if you run across her, tell her I'm with Cynwrigg. We'll return here once we know something."

I linked with the owl. *"Your brothers and sisters are keeping something of mine."*

He fluffed his feathers and hooted softly. *"Would you like the papers, Regent?"*

"Aye. Please."

The owl launched from Ysir's shoulder and flew away. His hoots turned strident as he instructed his kin to bring the pages to me.

"What exactly did you give them?" Dariyah asked.

"The signature sheets for the new covenant," I told her. "You were there when it was happening."

"So I was. I'd forgotten."

"I should have been their keeper." Ysir stepped nearer, bristling with outrage. "All documents live in my library."

A smile wanted out. I held it in check and longed for a world as black and white as his. "You weren't here. Had you been, of course I'd have given them to you for safe-keeping."

Owls converged from every direction with sheets of paper clutched in their beaks. I collected everything, thanking each bird as it released its burden into my hands. My intent had been to take the covenant with me to Dubrova. Instead, I gave the documents to Ysir.

He smoothed the corners and places beaks had punched holes in the paper, clucking over the stack of pages. "You should use better vellum, Regent. Not this cheap substitute."

"Certainly," I murmured, not having the heart to tell him vellum had fallen out of fashion. The animals rights' activists would have had a heyday protesting the use of hides when pulp held so many advantages.

"Normally, I'd file them with the other covenant versions in their special spot in the library," Ysir spoke slowly. "Where would you like me to keep them until they can be returned to their rightful location?"

"Wherever they will be safe," I told him and built a spell to bring us close to Dubrova. The unicorns' extended silence had shifted from worrisome to a dull space in my mind brimming with dread.

"I shall take care of them." Ysir turned and shambled back toward the depths of the grove where he'd been when we arrived.

"Should we bring reinforcements?" Dariyah asked.

It was tempting, but I wanted to see what we faced. If things were as desperate as I feared, I didn't want to drag anyone else into it until I had a better idea what we were up against. The Unseelie were warriors. For the most part, we weren't.

"Not yet," I replied. "You manage a ward, I'll get us close to the castle, but on the back side because it's less used."

The bite of her magic snapped around me. She built a ward and then cobbled it together with my power to make it bulletproof. The rolling hills behind the castle took shape. The first thing I noticed was absolute silence. Faery is usually alive with small noises. Not here, though.

"This doesn't feel right," Dariyah breathed near my ear.

It didn't to me, either. I put a finger in front of my mouth to signal a need for total quiet and led the way around the bulk of the castle toward the front. A double line of unicorns faced a row of Unseelie warriors. Both had been frozen in place. No wonder it was so fucking silent.

Dariyah nudged me and turned her hands palms up. I offered a shrug in return. She wanted to know who'd had enough power to manage the forced stalemate. I had no idea.

Dubrova's front door stood open. If anyone was

within orchestrating the odd tableau, I couldn't see them, so I let my gaze travel upward. If I wanted to expend a lot of power, the best vantage point is always from above. Magic can defy gravity, but you get more bang for your buck when you're going with the flow.

Dariyah pointed about the time I saw the King of Winter standing on a parapet next to a white winged horse with a snowy mane who had to be Pegasus. Born of Poseidon and Medusa, the horse had been steeped in evil since his inception. Being this close to both of them —Dariyah and Pegasus—was complicated, but the magical feel of the two was so close it was eerie.

I'd been dead wrong about who I'd assumed her father was. He was poised above us. Did he know Auril had borne his seed? A hasty glance at Dariyah suggested she didn't share my revelation. Auril had done an excellent job making certain she'd never find her father on her own.

"I thought Pegasus was decent," Dariyah mouthed.

I shook my head. The mythical horse had been idealized in modern legends, but the truth was far darker. No one embraced the winged steed any more than they welcomed the monster I'd been certain had fathered her. I hadn't released my teleport spell, so I directed us back to the glade.

Ysir didn't wander out to greet us; I honed seeking magic hunting Auril and Titania. It didn't go well. My casting boomeranged back in my face. "Can you find your mother?" I kept my voice low in case Ysir was nearer than I thought.

"Of course. What the hell was that back there?"

"Pegasus must be the force behind the King of Winter. Whether Oberon knows about him or not is anyone's guess."

"I'm confused. Pegasus isn't supposed to be wicked," Dariyah murmured.

"Think again. He's as evil as they come. Medusa was his mother. The other Gorgons are his aunts."

"And Poseidon is his father. I get that part, but I've never considered the ramifications. Walk this way. Mother isn't far. I can't sense Titania, but I bet they're together."

I hurried after Dariyah and shuffled through options. Just saying Pegasus was at Dubrova might be enough, but Dariyah had a right to know who her father was. If we confronted him, she'd find out anyway. Pegasus would recognize his own, and it could fall out several ways from him being delighted to swooping down and pounding Dariyah to a pulp with his sharp hoofs.

Beyond all that, why had Auril chosen him to create a child? She must have seen something in a vision. No one would be a willing consort to the winged steed. Legends suggested he turned into a man at will, a deadly beautiful one with white-blonde hair and eyes like the sea. No mortal woman could resist him, and he killed them after he'd taken his pleasure.

"Take no prisoners," I muttered.

Dariyah glanced at me. "What?"

"Never mind. How much farther."

"We're there." Power shot from her hands, and the earth beneath us dropped away. We didn't fall very far and landed in front of a gate crafted of abalone shells probably culled from Faery's sea.

Before I could study the problem of urging the gates to open, Auril strode through with Titania next to her. "Good to see you," she said brusquely.

"Is it?" Dariyah squared off in front of her.

"Aye, daughter. Must you always hunt for unpleasantness beneath the most neutral statement?"

"Not now," I said sharply enough all three women stared at me. I focused my next words at Auril. "Pegasus and the King of Winter are at Dubrova. They've put both their own troops and my unicorns in thrall."

"For what purpose?" Titania demanded.

"Probably because the Unseelie were losing," I said, followed by, "It's time."

"What you mean," Auril retorted, "is that mine finally ran out."

"What in the fuck are the two of you talking about?" Dariyah asked. "Seems like now would be when we pony up troops and take back the castle."

Auril already stood toe to toe with her daughter. "Good you're feeling that way," she said, "because you're the only one of us who has a fighting chance against Pegasus."

"Bullshit!" I thundered. "You are not going to pit Dariyah against that monster. I forbid it."

But no one was paying me the slightest heed.

"Why me?" Dariyah's voice could have etched glass.

"Because, child, he is your father."

Finally. The cards were face up on the table. I wasn't certain what I'd expected, but it wasn't Dariyah's face twisting into a disgusted scowl. "How could you?" she demanded.

"I did what I had to," Auril replied in an even tone. "Everything, even this, was foreordained. I didn't see exactly how it would play out, but now that we're here, you will do your part."

"The fuck I will. Find yourself another patsy. I don't owe Faery shit. Or you, either." The air around Dariyah glistened, turned red, and enveloped her as she vanished.

"What are you waiting for?" Titania snapped her fingers in front of my face. "Go after her. Bring her back."

Auril shook her head. "It wouldn't do any good. Destiny has a way of finding us. We can't force it down her throat."

"In the meantime," I said acidly, "I'm up for

suggestions. Since you seem to know our primary adversary, Auril, let's begin with you."

Concern for Dariyah nipped at me, but I shoved it aside. At least she was safe for the moment. I'd marshal Faery's resources and do my damnedest to oust the usurpers.

Could we do it absent a direct link with the land?

I suspected not, but we were in the thick of things. No way out but through.

12

CHAPTER TWELVE, DARIYAH

By the time the walls of my new flat solidified around me, I was sobbing and furious. Crying was stupid. It wouldn't solve anything. I had to get hold of myself. Midnight launched his furry body through the open window and into my arms. I sank onto the floor and held him for so long the quality of light leeching through the cheap drapes changed enough to tell me it would soon be dark.

Faery and Earth ran on independent timelines since night had long since fallen there. I'd run out of tears a while back, but my mind pedaled in weary circles. I needed a plan. Somewhere to go. Something to do.

Part of me was screaming Cynwrigg needed me, and I should hurry back to Faery. Another part never wanted to lay eyes on Mother again. She'd schemed and plotted and used me—her own flesh and blood—for some nefarious end. Probably, she'd seen today in many iterations.

Was the only reason she'd birthed me, nurtured me, to send me into a macabre battle against the other half of my bloodline? Shit. I'd fallen into a bad rendition of a Greek tragedy, but nowhere was it written I couldn't scramble out of the pit. In my world, I had free will. I got to pick and choose where I went, what I did, whom I associated with.

"Yeah, there it is." My voice was dead, dull, rustling like desiccated leaves. I sounded so odd, even the cat stopped purring. Choices shaped up like the spokes of a wheel circling me. I could return to my old life, the only one I'd known since leaving Mother. A couple of hundred years before, I'd have hired out as a hedge Witch hawking charms and cures for whatever ailed you. In today's world, I'd hit the registry, search for a job—preferably one located far from here—and keep on keeping on.

It would preserve the illusion of being mistress of my own ship. But for how long? Even with my skimpy magical education—eh, maybe not skimpy so much as titrated—Mother had done a bang-up job teaching me the things she wanted me to learn. One of those lessons had been about destiny.

"You can run, but you can't hide. Not forever," I muttered.

It turned the question of the hour into what I wanted to do right now, this minute. Did I return to Faery and lend my magic to fight for a land that had done nothing for me? Or did I visit the registry first thing tomorrow and go back to work. I'd pick a new glamour and maybe another name. Cats don't care for change, but I'd bring Midnight with me. He'd chosen to remain in the new flat rather than returning to the old one, which proved he'd settle in.

That path held a certain appeal, but walking out on Cynwrigg felt wrong on so many fronts. I was falling in love with him. Appalled by a significant chink in my armor, I backed away from the thought. How had I lowered my guard enough to let something like that even happen? Not that it mattered. Can't stuff some genies back into bottles, and this was one of them.

I couldn't unlove him. And it would be a long time before I stopped thinking about him, if I ever did. What if something happened to him without my magic to blend with his? Was that the trap that would lure me back? Worry that my selfishness would be his undoing chipped away at me.

He's been taking care of himself for a long while, I told myself, recognizing it for the weak suck excuse it was. Cyn had, indeed, been on his own, but never under such challenging circumstances. He was regent. The fate of his land and his people were his responsibility. He'd go the distance, do whatever it took to free Faery from evil.

His dedication made me feel small and petty. The only one I'd ever looked after was me—and a series of pets like Midnight. Nothing wrong with my instincts. I wasn't stingy. When I was someplace I could do good, I didn't dither about the pros and cons, I acted.

Like when I'd become Faery's agent to heal her rift or when I'd plucked a dead unicorn's last thoughts from her mind, so we'd know more about how she died. Reaching beyond myself had felt proper, pure even.

What was my stumbling block now? Not Cynwrigg. Nope, it was Mother. If she knew a storm was brewing—never mind how many hundreds of years in the future—she should have prepared me. At least given me the information I'd need to watch out for certain things.

It ran deeper than "should." It had been her duty to impart basic knowledge. I scootched over so I could lean against a wall with Midnight still in my arms. The cat had fallen asleep, but was still purring like a little dragon. The dead weight of the sleeping feline was comforting and buffered the illusion I wasn't alone.

I squeezed my eyes shut for a moment. They felt gritty from my spate of tears. Lying to myself has never been my style. No reason to begin now. The bald truth was I'd been alone since I walked away from the distant world where Mother and I had lived. Mining deeper, I'd been alone there too. Mother was often absent for lengthy periods. Her body may have been there, but the rest of her had been deep in some trance or other.

After I hit a certain age, I understood not to disturb her unless the sky was falling. Since it never was, I became adept at existing with only myself for company. Breath rattled from me, but my chest didn't feel as constricted. I hadn't been a child for eons. Mother was who she was. She'd done what she felt she had to. It wasn't as if she'd had any more of a sounding board than I'd possessed. Although, most of her monumental choices had occurred before she left Faery.

The sad part was we could have been there for each other. If she'd trusted me. Understanding dawned she'd never transitioned from viewing me as a child, as an inferior both intellectually and magically. Maybe closer to the mark, she'd feared the form Pegasus's contribution to my power would take once it was fully matured.

Her way to deal with it was to keep me on a short leash. I'd asked her about various castings many times only to be told we'd get back to them. Except we never did. I didn't know if she figured I'd forget or what.

I'd never realized the extent she'd gone to shape me. It had worked because in the end keeping the peace meant more to me than having my way. There were only the two of us, and our remote outpost turned chilly and inhospitable when Mother rebuked me or withdrew herself for days at a time.

My mouth curved into half a smile. I'd always seen myself as totally independent, self-sufficient, and an introvert. Maybe I wasn't quite as need-free as I'd always imagined. A brisk walk might be the ticket to clear my muddled thoughts. It was full dark outside, and I was a master at escaping notice. If I ended up returning to Faery, it should be sooner rather than later. If I tarried too long, I might not arrive in time to do anything but pick up the pieces—and kill the bastard who'd fathered me.

Every life has an overarching purpose. If this was mine, I needed to own it, not run from it. Damn Mother, anyway. Information, any at all, would have been nice. No wonder I'd had vestigial wing buds as a child, except they hadn't been from a Sidhe. Or a dragon.

I set the sleeping cat down, told him I'd be back soon, and let myself out the door. A blast of still-hot air reminded me to shuck my jacket and drop it back inside. Faery might be temperate. Reno wasn't. Not in the summertime.

I didn't employ magic for this jaunt. If any other mages were out and about, I didn't want to draw attention to myself. I was fairly certain Oberon had removed his stooges. Even if he hadn't, they were stationed miles away. He'd be fully engaged with the tableau unfolding in Faery, too busy to worry about me. Regardless how pissed he was about Titania's rescue, he had bigger fish to fry. Did he know Pegasus had crashed Faery's gates?

Eh, he'd almost have to. The enchantment cascading off the winged steed had been too robust to ignore. Now that the blinders were off, I cringed. How in the hell had I missed blood calling to its own?

I shook my head and looked around the full-ish parking lot wondering which direction would yield the highest chance of solitude. Having decided on a park a few blocks away, I settled into an easy lope.

I'd missed the siren call of Father's blood because of something Mother had done. She'd disabled the part of my power that would have picked up on the connection immediately. She'd done it on purpose, but why? Certainly not to cripple my reactions. That level of trickery didn't fit her personality.

Her rationale had likely been more self-serving and immediate. Probably, she'd wanted to stave off explana-tions for as long as possible. She'd have to be embar-rassed, but she'd pushed beyond the personal and taken one for the team.

Yeah, nice try, my inner critic noted dryly. "Team" suggested batting on the same side and all that. She'd never given me a chance to sign up, or even see if I wanted to. That wasn't a team but a one-woman show where Mother called all the shots, and I remained in the dark.

What was it with her unfortunate choices of mates? The King of Winter was looking like quite the piece of work, and I'd make a point of reading up on Pegasus if I ever got back to Ysir's carefully tended collection of books and scrolls. His material was bound to be more accurate than dialing up Google.

My pace slowed, and I kicked myself in the butt for being critical. It wasn't as if I hadn't invited my own share of losers to my bed. The big difference was they were all mortal and easy to get rid of. Perhaps the Winter King had been an arranged liaison. They were quite common centuries back. And Pegasus had to be the result of one of her visions. She'd seen something and come back to it again and again. No matter how distasteful she found the message, she'd pitched in and done her part.

Sheesh. How had she felt about me? The child foisted onto her by fate. Likely not a discussion we'd ever have. She'd never tell me, anyway. Not so long as she viewed me as a child.

I'd reached the park and was jogging around its grassy verge. To keep anything green here required obscene infusions of water. Families sat at tables. A group of kids booted a soccer ball around. Dogs and kids and bikes crowded the verdant space.

I moved off to one side, putting distance between myself and everyone else. No one paid me the slightest bit of attention, and it suited my mood fine. I didn't belong here. I never had. I'd made the best of a crappy situation, one foisted onto me by default. Faery had been closed to me. The mostly deserted other worlds held little appeal. If I was going to choose one of them, I may as well have remained with Mother.

And so, I'd ended up on Earth. Done my best to blend in and pass for human. The blending-in part hadn't been necessary until maybe 150 years ago. Before then, mortals still believed in magic, and I could be a Witch or a crone or any of a number of magelike creatures. Hell, I'd even done a stint masquerading as a Banshee, and another as Cailleach. Until she'd found out and been so angry, I'd figured my time was up.

Chuckling to myself, I remembered her tirade. She'd come out with her guns blazing—and left just as quickly. I bet she'd figured out who my father was, and it had been just the wakeup call to chase her away.

My decision wasn't really one at all. It boiled down to being an outsider and on the run forever or claiming my rather shaky spot in Faery—if such a thing existed. If my sole purpose was to defeat Pegasus and return Faery to its rightful leaders, would there be a place for me at the end of the fighting?

A line from *Lord of the Rings* flared through my mind.

The one about Frodo saving Middle Earth but not for him. Was I destined to save Faery and then be banished from it?

I rolled my mental eyes, told myself to buck up, and got to my feet. Mother was who she was. She'd never change. Either I accepted her or walked away from her forever. After the battle was done, she'd still have her Midnight Court. Whether I could carve out my own niche in Faery remained to be seen.

Would Cynwrigg be a part of...well, of anything? Our magic was destined to work in sync, and being near him made me long for something I'd never had. A man to share my life with. Wanting and having were two different things, though. I could weave pleasant fantasies about us living happily ever after, but fantasy endings are just that: not real.

Not for me, anyway. And maybe not for anybody magical. Not too many storied legends of love amongst immortals. Keeping a flame burning through a human lifespan was at least theoretically feasible. Keeping it going through forever seemed impossibly remote.

One thing at a time. I was nearly back to my flat. I let myself in, locked the door behind me, and sat next to Midnight. He hadn't moved, but he was awake with his eyes focused on me. I used telepathy because I thought it might transmit my thoughts better.

"I love you," I told the cat. *"I have to leave. There's a*

chance I won't be back. Feel free to come and go as long as this place is empty. If someone else moves in, you're better off near the old house."

He stalked to me and rubbed his body against my ribs. I stroked his soft fur and sent a prayer to the goddess I'd come through whatever lay in my future. I didn't want this to be a forever goodbye. After climbing up my body and swiping his sandpaper tongue across my neck, he jumped down, trotted to the window, and slipped out into the night.

No more excuses. Time for me to go too. I culled through my clothes and grabbed a few things I might need, changing into clean black pants before teleporting to the stairs under Lady Luck. It was a short walk from there through the boundary separating Earth from Faery's enchanted realm.

As I'd traveled, an idea took shape. Rather than heading up, I moved down, farther into the space beneath Faery. I wanted to talk with the land, see if what I'd been toying with had a chance in hell of working without killing me in the process.

The cavern beneath Faery formed around me. The odd light in this place made the crystals shimmer in an array of delicate colors. "Are you here?" I asked softly.

One stone plopped in front of me. I smiled. Faery remembered the method we'd employed to communicate last time. Not trusting how magic traveled through the roots of Faery, I switched to telepathy in old Gaelic and shielded my message as best I could.

What I was suggesting would require more than yes-no answers from her, but we'd come this far. I trusted we'd figure things out. Stones fell. It took a moment before I understood they formed a line. Riding a hunch, I followed it to the edge of the cave and an indentation I hadn't noticed. Magic was thick here, the scents of Faery dense and alluring. The same sense of coming home I'd had my first trip to Faery surrounded me

"Can you hear me, child?" whooshed through my head like an unquiet breeze.

"Yes." I tucked myself into the crystal-lined hollow as closely as I could. The stones were sharp, but not intolerable.

"Excellent. I was hoping this would work. What you proposed carries severe risk to you."

I'd figured as much, but details would be useful. *"Go on,"* I said.

What she told me wasn't much worse than I'd imagined. More permanent, but not worse. *"Let's do this,"* I told her. I've always landed on my feet. I had to believe this time wouldn't be any different.

"Return to your allies," Faery's rich voice went on. She sounded stronger than she had a few moments before. Perhaps the specter of battle energized her. *"Make your plans. I will know when they are complete."*

"You still hear everything, don't you."

"Aye, child, from everyone. It will offer us quite the edge because they can't throw any surprises our way."

Before I lost my nerve and said we needed to float lots more ideas to come up with viable ones, I walked from the cave and set a travel spell in place to bring me to the Midnight Court.

The glade was empty when my spell spit me out, but not for long. Cynwrigg ran toward me and pulled me to him so hard it stole my breath. Mother and Titania were right behind him.

"No time for that," Titania said sharply.

Cynwrigg ignored her. "I am so glad to see you," he said next to my ear.

"Same," I murmured, too tongue-tied to give voice to the array of emotions buffeting me. Whether what I'd just done had been my most courageous exploit or my stupidest remained to be seen.

"Thank you," he added. "We need your magic. We would have pressed forward without it, but our chances of success just shot upward."

I smiled, pleased by the compliment. "Hope your optimism isn't premature. I'm here because I want to be," I told him. "Some of my motivation isn't especially altruistic. I have to find a place for myself. Faery might not be it, but Earth isn't, either."

"I understand." He tucked my head into the hollow

between his neck and shoulder until I heard the solid beat of his heart. And then he let me go.

I turned to Mother and Titania. "I've worked out a plan with Faery," I told them.

Mother held up a hand. "Before we launch whatever we end up doing, I owe you an apology. Lots of them, actually. I hope we have time at the end of all this to get to know one another. I'm proud of you, of what you've made of yourself."

The tears I'd been certain I was done with sheened my eyes. I brushed them aside. "I hope the same," I told her.

"Now that we have the family drama laid to rest or at least under better control," Titania cut in, "let's get moving."

"Sounds as if you have plans in place," I said. "Tell me what they are."

Cyn nodded and began to talk. I reached for Faery, urging her not to miss any of this. Once our compact came together, my magic would be whole, but the rest of me would be merged with the land.

Cyn wouldn't like it, Mother wouldn't, either, but I'd made up my mind. It was our strongest play, and we'd be idiots not to take advantage of every shred of talent in our arsenal. We were playing for keeps. No second chances. If this didn't work, we might never regain Faery, and goddess only knew what plans the King of Winter had for it.

It hurt to think about Pegasus. So I didn't. What a rat-fuck. Most young girls would kill for a horse with wings in their family tree.

Yep, but I'm neither young nor most girls. Besides if they knew the truth about this horse, they'd run as far and as fast as they could from the shoddy reality.

"Dariyah?" Mother must have sensed my inattention because her tone held an edge.

"I'm listening," I told her. "Faery is too."

CHAPTER THIRTEEN, CYN

I felt Dariyah's magic before I saw her, and my spirits soared. I hadn't believed she'd come back. I should have restrained myself, but holding her shot to center stage, and I wrapped her in my arms. Dark smudges sat beneath her eyes, and she looked trashed. More than anything, I wanted to protect her, spirit her to somewhere safe, a place she could rest and wait out the coming battle.

Except it wasn't why she'd returned to Faery. She was here to add her magic to mine. To fight a war that wasn't rightfully hers. What had Faery ever done for her but make it abundantly clear she wasn't welcome here?

I'd fixed that problem with alterations to the covenant, but would any of us continue long enough to appreciate the new version? It wasn't a question I had an answer for. After Dariyah left, I'd expected at least a cursory explanation from Auril about her liaison with Pegasus.

She hadn't even skirted the topic. She'd ignored it. Instead, we'd tapped Ysir's extensive knowledge of history to construct a battle plan after I'd quizzed Auril about what outcomes her future-seeking had produced. I believed her when she said she'd seen so many outcomes to the war in Faery, the field was wide open.

A seer in his own right, Ysir had nodded in understanding. After patting Auril's shoulder, he'd gone to mobilize everyone he could find in Faery, and I didn't feel good about it. Most of Faery's inhabitants aren't warriors. They're good-hearted magical creatures, and today's events would scar them permanently. Friends would die in front of them.

Faery's lands would run red with blood.

I'd been lost in grim thoughts when Dariyah materialized. Her presence made it possible to push them aside. I'd just finished outlining what we planned to get Dariyah up to speed when Auril elbowed her daughter and spoke her name.

"I'm listening," Dariyah said. "Faery is too."

It was a curious add-on. Of course Faery could attend to everything that transpired here. It was her world. Still, Dariyah's statement ran deeper than face value.

"What do you mean?" I asked, hoping I was reading far too much into three small words.

Dariyah clasped her hands behind her back and stood tall. "I cut a deal with Faery. She will use my body, and—"

"I forbid it," Auril said flatly. "Last time, she nearly killed you."

Dariyah sent an indulgent glance her mother's way. "You have no say over my decisions. Motherhood only goes so far."

"But, child," Titania began.

Dariyah cut her off too. "The deal's been made. No going back. Faery is strong, ancient. This is her world. If anyone can wrest it from my fath"—she made a sour face—"from Pegasus and the Unseelie, it's her. But she has a fallback position if things aren't going well."

"And that is?" I asked.

Dariyah drew her brows together. "It's complicated, and I'm not certain I understand it fully, but the three of you might. If defeat seems certain, Faery will drag all of us behind some veil to a carbon-copy world. Then she'll withdraw every scrap of magic from this one. Absent power to extract, the original Faery will lose its appeal. No one will want it any longer, and then we can return."

"And start from scratch adding magic back in." Titania shook her head. "That would take half a century or more. And the only world that would accommodate us all is Fire Mountain. The dragons won't like it."

"Neither will we," Dariyah muttered. "That place is a hell hole."

"Never never let a dragon hear you say that. They adore their home." Auril shook a finger her way.

"Maybe not Fire Mountain," I said. "Other worlds exist within Faery's purview, but they all require magical awakenings."

"Not Fire Mountain," Auril said firmly. "This world, my world where I built and maintained the Midnight Court is the only logical choice."

It was a curious statement. I wanted to know more, but we couldn't think about where we'd end up if things didn't go well. "We can't deal with any of that now," I pointed out. "Our focus has to be here. On winning, not losing." Turning to Dariyah, I asked, "How will blending our magic happen when Faery is working through you?"

"My magic should be intact." She smiled crookedly. "I'm thinking maybe a three-for-one deal. You. Me. Faery. Seems unbeatable."

"I like your attitude. Does Pegasus know about you?"

She shrugged and hooked a thumb Auril's way. "Ask her."

"Nay. He does not."

"Will he recognize her?" I pressed for clarification.

"Probably not if her essence is subsumed by Faery,"

Auril answered slowly.

"Any idea how he'll react if you're wrong?" I crooked two fingers her way.

Auril opened her mouth, closed it, and started over. "No idea. I came to him deeply disguised. He'd adopted his mortal form, assumed I was human, and tried to kill me afterward. I snared him in a sleeping spell and made my escape."

"You're stronger than him magically?" It was a good point to clarify.

"I don't believe so. I caught him unaware while he was mixing a potion to poison me. Not that the night-shade would have had any effect, but he didn't know."

The stiff set to Dariyah's shoulders relaxed a little. Perhaps knowing her mother's liaison with the horse had been a one-time event made it more palatable. It did for me.

People and animals had begun streaming into the glade. What was once a joyous site full of hope and revelry had turned into a staging area for a battle that might spell the end of Faery. While it was encouraging the land had a plan B, the logistics of executing it seemed hazy.

What in the goddess's name was wrong with me? If I didn't stay on top of them, my thoughts devolved into a bleak pit. It wasn't like me at all. Everything in Faery is intertwined. Between Dubrova being under siege,

Oberon's treachery, and Pegasus's presence, evil dragged at me.

Portals opened disgorging dragons. Excellent. I'd hoped they wouldn't swoosh through the skies announcing their presence. Ysir had done a most exceptional job, considering his only acquaintance with battle strategy was via poring over scrolls.

The old librarian walked toward me, steadier on his feet than he had been. "All are assembling, Regent, as you requested."

"You missed your calling," I told him. "You could have commanded armies."

He cracked a rare smile. "That's the thing about immortality. I might do that one of these days. Oh. The serpents. I had them teleport to the sea. Didn't seem as if they'd be safe remaining in the moat."

"Good call."

He shrugged. "I want my library back. Before those intruders move everything, and it takes years to set the place to rights."

I didn't bother to mention the "intruders" were more likely to torch his precious library than anything else. Shuttling documents from one place to another was probably low on their list.

Dragons were forming battalions. I beckoned to Auril, Titania, and Dariyah, and we talked briefly with each of the four dragons who were leading troops into battle. My message was the same for them all. Protect life wherever possible—on our side. A glance at the nymphs and satyrs and Fae and Sidhe and all the varieties of animals hurt my heart. Some clutched magical accoutrements; some carried plain, garden-variety weaponry. Most were empty-handed. Birds circled overhead.

"Are other dragons coming?" I asked a large red-scaled fellow.

He shook his head. "We sent what we thought was necessary. No one told us we'd face Pegasus. That infernal mother of his is sure to show up. She's always coddled him. And don't forget her sisters."

Breath whooshed from me; a kick in the guts wouldn't have been more of a surprise. The dragon had suggested we'd face Medusa with her writhing headful of venomous snakes. And the other Gorgons. It wasn't good news. At all. Besides, I'd thought Medusa dead at Perseus's hands. Often, though, the immortal don't remain dead for long.

"Can you request reinforcements?" I asked the dragon.

"Already done." Steam and smoke spooled from his open mouth.

I lowered my voice. "Do you suspect the Shadow Lords might be involved?"

A stream of fire shot from his mouth and he

shrugged amid rattling scales. When he replied, he'd switched to telepathy. *"Best to not even think their names."*

Night—the first one in memory—was ceding to day. It was almost time. Titania marched at the head of one group, Auril another. At the time we'd developed this plan, I'd planned to lead the other two groups to the castle gates. Titania would cover the rear, and Auril's team would take the side fronting the moat.

One of our first tasks was to break the spell holding the unicorns in stasis. Of all Faery's citizenry, they were our staunchest warriors. Dariyah ran to my side. "I can't hold her back much longer. If this doesn't work, and I lose myself, I love you."

Something deep inside me twisted at words I'd longed to hear. "Thank you, but why tell me now?"

"I might not get another chance."

I held her close. "It has to work. Don't fight her. That way, you'll have a better chance of breaking free."

"Already thought of that. We have to believe she means well and won't want to hang onto me."

I nodded and whispered, "I love you too. Fight well," before I let her go. I feared the clarion call of having a body would be too much for Faery to walk away from. I'd meant to ask Ysir about the era when she'd been corporeal, but now there wasn't time.

I looked for him and said, "Your task is done. Find a safe vantage point."

"Aye, Regent. I shall do all in my power to add magic where 'tis required."

Power flared around each group as they prepared to teleport into position. Dariyah's body took on an insubstantial aspect. When it reshaped, magic spilled from her, and I felt the bite of Faery's presence. We'd timed our attack to mesh with the dawn. Dubrova rose before me in all its shining glory; the castle was dimmer than before but still magnificent. Determination rocked me. I'd be damned if I'd stand by while an Unseelie horde took over the seat of Faery's power.

Dragons bugled; a horse screamed overhead. Heh. The dragons would give Pegasus a serious run for his money. The unicorns were right where I'd last seen them, frozen in place. The Unseelies who'd been ranged across from them were gone. Of course, the King of Winter would have taken care to free his men. It must have absorbed more time than he'd counted on, or the unicorns would be dead.

Shouting a spell I'd conjured earlier, the shrouding around the unicorns reacted to my casting and grew visible. Once they could see it, two dragons shot holes in its weave with jets of flame until the nasty structure fell away. I kept my chant going in case something I couldn't see still bound them. They certainly weren't moving although their prison no longer held them in place.

Dariyah darted forward. I motioned to a dragon to

cover her movements with fire. Meantime, something elemental shifted within me. The spot where Dariyah's power married with mine grew rich, varied, intricate. I sensed Faery and Dariyah and myself in the mix.

A language I didn't recognize rolled from Dariyah. The unicorns shook themselves and stamped their hoofs. I might not know the words, but their inflection was clear. She was urging them to get moving. They were sitting ducks in front of castle gates that could blow open at any moment. Someone had sealed them since I'd done my reconnaissance.

Faery is many things, but patient isn't part of her makeup. She and Dariyah flew through the air, landed on one of the unicorns, and cantered across the cobblestoned courtyard and through a gateway. After a pause long enough the dragon chivied the remaining ones with blasts of smoky ash, the herd wheeled and followed Faery's steed.

I'd have celebrated, but we'd barely gotten past step one. Shouting to both battalions, I led the charge as we surged forward. Above my head an aerial battle raged between Pegasus and a dragon. I couldn't take my attention off the gates for long, but it looked like a stalemate. The dragon hit the horse with fire, but it smoldered and died. The horse kicked the dragon in the head with hideously sharp hoofs. The dragon made a grab for an offending hoof, and the whole thing started over again.

A group of Sidhe were cycling through spells to get the castle gates to open. Why weren't the King of Winter and his minions barreling through? It wasn't like him to hide. The Sidhe spell rose in volume until the fine hairs on the back of my neck stood on end.

Everyone behind us was vulnerable. Hell, we all were. I'd read accounts of troops crushed between something like Dubrova and oncoming hordes. Was that why no one was blasting out of the castle?

I might be wrong, but suddenly remaining in place seemed like the wrong approach. It was what our adversary was counting on, and predictability could spell ruin.

I whistled shrilly and turned us around. *"To me!"* I directed mind speech at the other groups and set a rapid pace until we were on the rolling land outside the castle gates. It was counterintuitive. We wanted to reclaim the castle. It was the other way, but holding our previous position meant we could have been crushed like rats.

"But we almost had the door open," a Sidhe told me.

I had no answer for him. Almost wasn't good enough, and even if the door had opened, we'd have been just as trapped. If it were me within, I'd have boobytrapped the place from now till next week.

Thundering hoofs announced the unicorns had found their minds again and were barreling toward us. Dariyah/Faery still perched atop one of them, but she jumped down when they got close.

How was she holding up? A magical scan would probably annoy Faery. Dariyah was correct. We had to believe in her good intentions. A mix of magics turned the air into a simmering brew of unpleasant sensations. I'd made the right choice after all, getting us into the open.

Bugles, roars, growls, and snarls presaged a ragtag group of animals and misshapen humans. They looked like a mad scientist had gone nuts and mixed DNA as the mood struck him. Four-legged wolf-cougar blends had more teeth than either animal alone. They stood as tall as most horses. One took a swipe at a unicorn's hock. Quick on his feet, the unicorn twisted midair and landed a solid kick. The wolf's head shattered. Blood geysered everywhere.

The stench of death and decay joined the twisted magic, creating a noxious stew that made me glad I hadn't eaten recently. Dragons shot fire from above. Too bad there weren't a few more of them. I feinted hard right to avoid something with wings and huge open jaws that had been aiming at my head. A thin stream of magic cut its head off, and it fell like a stone, splattering me with black ichor that stank like rotten onions.

Any pretense of an organized attack had fallen by the wayside. We were fighting what showed up in front of us. Jess raced past. I caught her up and told her to make certain the smaller animals went to ground. They had no place in this fight. Not with new monstrosities bearing down on us with each passing moment.

I'd already felt several raccoons and rabbits die. The thought caught me by surprise. It meant somehow my link to Faery's inhabitants had been restored. Had Oberon outlived his usefulness? Seemed like the most likely explanation, but I couldn't think about it now.

Bodies piled up until I had a hell of a hard time seeing what was going on. One of the unicorns cantered by. I jumped onto her back. "Sorry. I can't tell what's happening."

She didn't answer, just kept on running and goring everything in our path. More dragons had shown up. They mowed a path through the wicked, but a few innocents were snared in their fire too. If Oberon wasn't dead already, I'd twist his head from his body.

If he hadn't been so arrogant and pigheaded, none of this would have come to pass. I hoped he was watching from some tower, horrified by the destruction he'd spawned.

Like the unicorn, I fought mindlessly. Sight. Kill. Avoid whatever launched itself at me. Rinse and repeat.

Dariyah/Faery crossed my field of vision from time to time. I kept expecting us to make a dent in the warped hordes, but for every one we killed, two more rose up to take their place. How was it possible?

"There's a hole," I muttered. "Has to be. A

passageway to another dimension."

"Or to Hell," the unicorn whinnied.

A discordant noise started from the direction of the castle, growing in intensity until I shielded my ears with magic. *"Follow me,"* Faery commanded. My unicorn companion must have heard her too because we wheeled and galloped hard for the gates around Dubrova.

They slammed shut behind us. Fuck. Had I just ridden into a snare set just for Faery, Dariyah, and me? The hideous rending grated against my ears. Glass breaking and grinding against itself with stones in the mix to amplify the noise.

Dubrova's front doors slammed against their stops. Two winged horrors launched through them. Pegasus and a woman who had to be Medusa. I'd never met her, but the corona of writhing snakes was a dead giveaway. Dariyah/Faery jumped down from the unicorn and swatted the beast on the rump. He wasn't having any of it. He turned, horn lowered, prepared to fight.

Power sheeted from Faery, forming a whirling vortex of spinning knives. Neat trick but Pegasus and Medusa had taken to the air, shrieking and howling like a pack of Banshees. The draw on my power intensified as Dariyah/Faery opened the spigot. I could give that much, but not for very long.

Jumping from the unicorn, I bolted toward Dariyah/Faery. Before I got there, Medusa swooped low.

Her eyes spun like dragons' eyes, but if anyone—magical or otherwise—looked at her, those whirling eyes turned them to stones.

Magic exploded in a rain of red sparks. Medusa reached through Dariyah/Faery's curtain of knives and flew off with her prey dangling from her hands.

"Nooooooo," I shrieked.

The place I'd been connected to them slammed shut with such force I fought to remain upright. I didn't have wings, but the dragons did. Summoning my shredded power, I landed on the nearest one's back. "Follow them," I shouted.

For a scant moment, I expected him to refuse. I might be regent, but the dragons didn't answer to me. Or anyone. "It only looks like Dariyah," I said. "She's one and the same with Faery right now."

The dragon heeled around, almost unseating me in the process, and took off after Medusa's fading figure. Auril flew into view on another dragon, hellbent on making Medusa sorry she'd ever become a goddess. I set magical markers, getting the feel of Medusa's power so we could track her even if she vanished on us. I wasn't under any illusions; my magical link had been severed because Medusa was throwing a very private party, one I hadn't been invited to.

I kept reminding myself Dariyah wasn't in this alone, but it didn't make me feel any better. Auril pulled slightly ahead. "Do you know where they're going?" I shouted.

"I think so."

I waited, but in true Auril form, she didn't add to her words. I felt torn. I should be leading my people, clearing the fuckers out of Dubrova, but I couldn't stand by while Dariyah was hijacked by a death-dealing goddess.

Why was I thinking this into the ground? I'd made my choice. The sooner I got Dariyah back, the sooner I could return to the raucous fray fanning out half a league on all sides of the castle. I'd been right about a passageway. Now that I was high enough, I saw it disgorging monsters.

"Tell your kin to shut that," I told the dragon.

"One step ahead of you...Regent."

The sky ahead flickered ominously. The spot Medusa had been closed over as if it had never been there. "It's a gateway," I said. "Go through it."

"Not sure we can," the dragon muttered as we ran up against something solid and almost fell out of the sky.

Auril and her dragon circled back to us. Apparently, the barrier didn't extend but a few meters in each direction. "Is your magic your own again?" she demanded. At my nod, she barreled into me. No grace. No subtlety. She commandeered my power and focused it at the place we'd lost sight of Dariyah/Faery.

CHAPTER FOURTEEN, DARIYAH

I didn't exactly have a ringside seat—things are fuzzy when Faery is in control—but even I knew when Medusa grabbed us by the hair. Faery's fury was palpable; so was the jolt when my—our—connection to Cyn was obliterated. I hoped to hell Faery had a plan because in my current state, I was helpless.

My scalp tingled and ached. Who would have guessed hair would be so resistant to simply breaking and falling away? Talking wasn't especially easy, but I had to try. *"Teleport us the fuck out of here,"* I squealed.

"Can't." Faery's terse reply told me just how much shit we'd landed in.

We passed through some kind of barrier. It burned and stung like fury, adding to the pain from my poor abraded scalp. Medusa was taking us somewhere. Did she know she'd nabbed Faery too? Or did she think she only had me? A faint thought took shape. I was her granddaughter. Surely, it would count for something.

Maybe. But it could backfire spectacularly too.

"We are heading for Sarpedon Island," Faery said.

I wanted to ask why there, but it was too much trouble. If the island was where I thought, it lay off Turkey's Aegean coast. Medusa may have made her home there a couple of thousand years ago, but that whole area was overrun with people today.

"I must return to my land," Faery went on. *"It is under siege. You're resourceful. You'll figure something out."*

If I'd thought the pain was bad before, it was nothing compared with the wrenching, tearing sensation that made me feel as if I'd been torn in two. Looking down, I expected my entrails to be hanging in the void.

They weren't.

At least my mind was my own again, and I'd moved past one dilemma.

I'd have laughed if everything didn't hurt so much. The problem that had solved itself was separating from Faery. She'd decided I was more of a liability than an asset and made the choice for us. But I'd wager it ran deeper than that. Much deeper. Faery had been scared. I'd felt her fear, smelled it, tasted it. She wanted nothing to do with Medusa, and so she'd left me to my fate.

What else would I have expected? We only honor

alliances that benefit us. Mine had run its course, but if she ever asked to share my body again, the answer would be a resounding no.

Not just no, but hell to the no.

The emptiness we'd been hurtling through exploded around us. White sand stretched beneath a painfully blue sky. The salt smell of the sea was right, but nothing else fit. Nothing grew here. Birds didn't fill the sky, and the hum of insects was absent. The reflection of sun against water was almost as unpleasant as Fire Mountain had been. Almost. Medusa's unholy grip on my scalp released and I fell, tumbling end over end.

It's not the falling but the landing that hurts. In a mad scramble against seconds ticking past, I funneled enough magic to partially cushion my fall. I still hit hard, but not hard enough to break something. The sand was just as hot and unpleasant as it looked. I crab-walked to my feet and turned to face Medusa.

She'd folded her black wings across her back. Her torso was naked but for a bronze torc wrapped around her neck. Something gauzy had been slung around her hips, and she was barefoot. Apparently, the blazing sand didn't bother her. Snakes coiled and uncoiled all around her head, hissing and spitting. I could smell the poison from where I stood, but didn't expect it would affect me.

The goddess settled hands tipped with long, black fingernails on her hips. "Something changed up there.

What?" Her voice was like listening to chalk scraping down a blackboard.

"Faery deserted a sinking ship," I said.

The goddess's spinning eyes widened. I'd heard you weren't supposed to look at her, but I didn't seem to be turning to stone. "Why would Faery borrow your puny body?" she asked.

"I offered it. Not as if she had many choices."

Medusa waved a dismissive hand. "Faery is dying. By the time we finish with it, nothing will be left. It's just as well. That place has outlived its usefulness."

"Tell that to everyone who resides there."

"I'd watch my words, girlie. You could lose your tongue."

I shoved my tangled hair behind my shoulders. Damn it to hell. My scalp still stung like a bitch, but if Medusa planned to kill me, I'd already be dead. Hell, she could have done me in back on Faery. Maybe. "Why am I here?" I asked.

"The King of Winter believes you're a problem. You and Cynwrigg ap Llyr freed Titania. She's nothing but trouble. Both kings had things well in hand until Titania and Auril returned."

I rolled my eyes. "Yeah? Tell me something I don't know. What I asked is why me?"

"I was curious what manner of being you were. I still can't quite tell."

If I'd been looking for a spot to deliver what she'd surely consider terrible news, I'd never get a better chance. "Look a little deeper, sweetie. I'm your granddaughter."

She fell back a step; the snakes all hissed in unison, their hungry mouths reaching my way.

"I should kill you on the spot for impertinence."

"Try it," I invited and raised my hands. Lightning bolts crackled from my fingertips.

"Pegasus has no spawn," she insisted. "Nor does Chrysaor."

"It's Pegasus. And none that he knows about," I said sweetly. "So long as we're onto a game of twenty questions, how it is you're alive. I thought Perseus beheaded you." My knowledge of mythology had returned along with my wits.

"He might have done that." She smiled menacingly. Blood dripped from her open mouth almost as if she'd turned into a Vampire, and a jagged scar grew visible under the torc. "I got even."

"I bet you did." Mirroring her position with hands on hips, I said, "What'll it be? You dragged me here. Your poison doesn't work on me. Neither do your eyes. Shall I teleport back to Faery and lend my magic to the battle raging there?"

A loud swooshing noise jerked my attention skyward but not for long. Crap. Who else was coming? If Medusa had ordered up reinforcements, I didn't want to hang around. Dealing with her was bad enough. And then I smelled Mother. And Cynwrigg. And dragons.

Medusa's gaze shot up. I wanted to look, but taking my eyes off her felt like a very bad idea. "Well, well, well." Medusa was almost purring. "I get three for the price of one abduction. Not a bad day's work."

Fire rained from the skies. One of the serpents fell off Medusa into a hissing, smoldering heap before bursting into flames. I wasn't sure quite what I expected, but she ignored her pet. Maybe they were as replaceable as beads in a necklace.

"Dariyah. Jump!" Cyn didn't bother with telepathy. It wouldn't have mattered if he had. Medusa could probably have intercepted it. I judged the distance between where I stood and the red dragon he rode and focused magic at the problem. It takes longer to tell about than it did to happen, but I was shackled to that infernal beach. No matter how hard I tried, I didn't budge. The rest of my power appeared to be online, working perfectly. But three tries convinced me Medusa had cut off any possibility of escape.

Mother and her blue dragon skidded in for a landing, churning the overheated sand until stinging bits scoured every inch of exposed flesh. I expected Mother to remain astride. It's what I would have done. Instead, she jumped down and strode to Medusa, remaining outside the range of the coiling snakes.

Medusa angled her head to one side; power flickered around Mother as the goddess hunted for information. Her face darkened, forehead forming a mass of lines. "You!" She pointed a long-nailed finger at Auril.

"Aye? Me, what?" Mother's expression could have chipped solid granite. It was her fuck-with-me-at-your-peril look.

Cyn and his dragon landed right next to me. I felt him latch onto my magic, but I still couldn't move more than a couple of square feet from where I stood. His booted feet hit the sand. He tested the barrier in multiple spots but couldn't reach me any more than I could get on the dragon. He switched to telepathy. *"What happened to Faery?"*

"She left before we got here."

He fisted a hand. *"Why that craven bitch. She abandoned you, and—"*

"Saved me the problem of her becoming too enamored of my body. It's all right."

Both beasts shot fire at Medusa, but she deflected the gouts of fiery ash and steam.

"You are her mother," Medusa ground out. Her words dragged my attention back to her cozy chat with Mother.

"Good to see your magic hasn't totally failed." Mother flashed a vicious grin.

"Why, you upstart bitch—" Medusa lunged, but Mother feinted beyond her reach.

"Thank about it," Mother went on, voice silkily smooth. "I'm her mother. Pegasus is her father. It means several things. For one, once the King of Winter discovers Pegasus not only had sex with me but created the child I'd denied him, their alliance should be all but finished."

"I'm not going to tell them." Medusa tossed her snake-filled head. Tails went flying as the serpents clambered for purchase.

"Aye, but I might."

"Not if I don't allow you to leave here."

Mother shaded her eyes with a hand and mimed looking around. When she dropped the hand to her side, she said, "How? There are three of us. And two dragons."

"These are my lands," Medusa retorted. "They answer to me."

Cyn quit trying to break through whatever barricade held me separate from him. "You don't want a dragon army here," he told Medusa, "and it's exactly what you'll end up with if you don't release us immediately. Besides, your precious son is under attack. Things aren't going well for him back at Dubrova. The unicorns we freed are out for his blood. At this very moment, he's on the ground. One of his wings has been severed, and—"

"You couldn't possibly know that," Medusa shrieked.

"Aye, but I could and do. I am regent to Faery. The land speaks to me. Calls to me. She left Dariyah to preserve her integrity, her wholeness."

I shuttered my mind. Cynwrigg had just tossed an outright lie into the mix. The land hadn't spoken to him —ever. Surely, Medusa would know and come down on him like a ton of bricks. Motion caught the corners of my eyes. A serpent had detached itself and slithered behind Mother.

"Behind you," I yelled and sent destructive power winging at the serpent's head. The dragons blasted it with fire.

Mother leapt high, but the serpent curved its body a foot above the sand. Its tongue flashed out and caught the side of her foot. Goddess be damned. Why couldn't she have worn shoes? The snake exploded in a fiery ball, but Mother's yelp told me the viper's strike had found its mark.

Panic has a place. It gave me what I needed to punch through Medusa's barricade. I wasn't elegant. I forgot all about complicated magical formulas. Using all my magic and all of Cyn's, I heaved everything in me at the barrier. It disintegrated in a flurry of black-barbed things. I was next to Mother in an instant, hands gripping her ankle to hold the venom at bay while I hunted for a magical antidote.

"There is no remedy," Medusa said smugly.

"Find one," Cyn thundered. "Or I swear, I'll finish what Perseus began." A long blade flashed into being, clutched in one of his hands. I remembered his knife that could take any form he wished. The dragons pounded the remaining serpents with fire until Medusa clutched at her head, tossing the burning snakes aside.

If she had replacements, they weren't in any rush to slink forward.

Mother was turning an unhealthy shade of gray. Despite my improvised tourniquet, red streaks edged up her leg. Power sheeted through her, and we worked together to defeat the toxin. Feeding magic into it seemed to add to its energy, no matter what element we led with.

Any anger I'd held onto frizzled to nothing. This was my *mother*. The only kin I had. I might not agree with how she'd done things, but I didn't want her to die because of me. She didn't have to come after me, but she had. Families are such a convoluted messy stew of feelings. Sorting them out now would be stupid. Perhaps ever sorting them would prove beyond me.

"Stop," I told Mother. "We have to think about this. Magic is making it worse."

"Aye." She was panting.

One of the dragons—the one Mother had ridden—trudged close. "I must open the wound. My fire will purify it and neutralize the venom."

I glanced up at his bulk. For some reason, his pinwheel-spinning eyes weren't as off-putting as before. His suggestion made sense, and I didn't have any better ideas.

"You must let go," he said, "or you'll lose your hands."

"If I do, the poison will spread faster." One glance at Mother's swollen mottled foot wasn't encouraging. Skin was already sloughing off around her toes; the acrid stench of poison stung my nostrils, and my hands had begun to tingle ominously.

"If you don't, it will kill her. Let go now." A thin stream of fire shot from the dragon's mouth with laser precision.

I released my hold the moment flames carved downward from a couple of inches above my grip. Mother's lower leg and ankle opened. Black ichor spewed from the wound and onto the burning sand.

"Sand," Mother wheezed.

I got the picture and grabbed handfuls of the heated grains, plastering them over the wound. They'd finish purifying whatever the dragon missed. Mother bit back a shriek. It began as a whistling moan that turned into a grunt. The foot-long gash must hurt like a bitch, but she grabbed more stand, stuffing it into the opening more vigorously than I would have.

I bit my lip so hard I tasted blood. Waiting was agonizing, but we'd done all we could. Had we been quick enough?

Mother's breathing, which had grown ragged, was stabilizing. Her color was better. No more black shit drained from the place the dragon had sliced her leg open. "Thank you," I told the dragon still hunched over us, more fire at the ready. "We did it."

"I believe we did," he bugled. "It was close. If you'd hesitated, I'd have sacrificed your hands."

"It would have been worth it." I bent to scrape sand out of the spots we'd dumped it.

"This is quicker," Mother said. Power swooshed, and the abrasion cleared of debris. Tissue and bone began knitting back together.

Cyn ran lightly to us. "Is Auril all right?" he asked.

"Yes. Thank the gods," I replied and looked up for the first time since I'd made a dive for Mother's ankle. Other than smoking snake carcasses, the beach was empty. "Where's Medusa?"

"She left." He'd sheathed his sword. "Guess she decided I was serious."

"Or she was worried about her poor widdle boy." Mother smirked and looked at Cynwrigg. "You lie brilliantly. What I don't understand is why Medusa didn't know you were lying to her."

"Truth nets must be cast before words fall," Cyn replied. "She was quick enough to toss one over me afterward, but the harm had been done."

"Help me up," Mother said.

I got a hand under one elbow. Cyn took the other, and we hauled her to her feet. She weighted the injured foot, grimaced, and said, "Eh, not as awful as I expected." Her gimlet gaze fell on me. "What happened to Faery?"

"She didn't want to tangle with Medusa. She didn't exactly say that. Her cover story was Faery needed her back sooner rather than later."

Mother shook a finger my way. "Next time..."

"There won't be a next time," I said before she launched into a spate of I-told-you-sos. "I'm not a spare set of clothes she can try on and discard at will."

The dragon who'd helped heal Mother settled his talons around her and gently lifted her onto his back. I understood the hint. We needed to get back before Medusa changed her mind and returned with an army of thugs.

"Do you mind if I ride behind her?" I asked the dragon.

"Not at all," he (she?) replied. How in the hell did you determine gender on dragons, anyway?

Cyn held me against him for a sweet, tender moment before letting go. He crawled up the other beast's scaly hide and dropped into position. I directed a bit of magic and settled behind Mother, wrapping my arms around her. "How are you doing?"

"By the time we get back to Faery, I'll be close to 100 percent."

I believed her. Her voice was strong again, her magic too. I took what I hoped would be my last look at Sarpedon Island. "How is this possible?" I asked.

"It's a parallel world," Mother said, clearly having understood I was asking how a deserted island could remain in the midst of a population explosion in the Middle East. "Medusa moved her base of operations long before the fall of Rome."

"Did you know her?"

"Vaguely." Mother twisted to look at me. "All that pantheon stuff is so much crap. The gods and goddesses just are. Different peoples called them by different names, but they're the same bastards and bitches no matter what name they carry."

She turned back around as the dragons' unique fire-based magical brew thickened around us. We were almost out of here. As the beach vanished, Mother continued. "Some of the deities, like Diana, are good illustrations of what I was just saying. She was Diana to the Romans, Artemis to the Greeks, and Arianrhod to the Celts. Medusa was in a class by herself, though. No one wanted to clone her or claim her."

Listening to Mother was so familiar and so bittersweet, my throat grew thick, and then I pulled my head out of my ass. We were a long way from out of the worst of things. Unless something unusual had happened, a battle still raged in Faery, one with a highly uncertain outcome.

I knew we were close because Faery's magic buffeted me. *"You're back. Let me in."*

"Fuck no."

"But why?" Insistence clutched at me, drilling holes in my resolve. I couldn't say no to Faery. I owed her allegiance. She was Mother to us all.

"Leave her alone," my real mother said firmly.

"Stay out of this, Auril." Faery's tone developed harsh edges.

"I will not stay out of it," Mother retorted.

The dogged presence clutching at me vanished. Getting rid of her couldn't be so simple. "Do you know what just happened?" I asked Mother.

"I do, but we're nearly there. Ready yourself. This won't be pretty."

Her words brought me up short. "Are you extrapolating from when you left?"

"No. I've finally seen enough about today to understand how this ends." She paused before adding. "The battle is lost. For now. We will retreat, lick our wounds, and find another way to prevail."

"But how could you know?" I persisted.

"When I look forward, the future shows itself to me in many, many versions. We've lived through enough of today for me to be fairly certain how it will end."

Cyn and his dragon passed out of the void. We followed them. Moments later, the glade where we'd prepared for battle spread before us. Bodies sprawled across the grassy swale as far as I could see. I'd assumed we'd return to Dubrova, but the dragons had been wiser than me.

Fae and Sidhe circulated among the fallen, tending to them. I draped Mother in magic and transferred us both to the ground. "We shall return to Fire Mountain," the dragon said.

"Aye, the other dragons left here a while ago," Cyn's mount added. "You know where to find us if you need us."

"Wait. Do you know what happened?" I cried, but the dragons took on an insubstantial aspect as their travel spell gelled around them.

"The other dragons who were here relayed events to him. He told me," Cyn said, his face lined with grief.

Mother nodded. "An Unseelie army, the likes of which no one imagined existed stormed Faery. Gargoyles joined them, and all the twisted creatures we saw emerging from that portal into Hell."

"They were too many"—Cyn picked up threads of the tale—"and Faery too weak. It didn't help that Oberon hogtied her by splitting her off from me. That part is done because the King of Winter sent Oberon packing."

"Please tell me he's dead," I cut in.

"I don't believe so," Cyn said.

"He may as well be. He's lost his mind," Mother said. "Which means the land should be there for the taking." Her implacable gaze fell on Cynwrigg.

He nodded briskly. "I'll give it a shot."

"I'd offer to ride along," I said, "but I just told her to piss up a rope. I'm probably not on her favorite person list at the moment."

"We have work to do here, Daughter." Mother took off at a brisk trot.

"Be careful," I told Cyn.

"I'll do the best I can," he murmured. "You'll be here?"

"If I have to leave, I'll let you know."

"Fair enough." He scanned the glade. "Even though Auril suggested as much, it never occurred to me we might have to fit all of Faery into the Midnight Court."

"Is it possible?"

"I wish I could answer that. I never paid enough

attention to how Auril constructed her exiled location to know much about it. But I will now."

I clasped his hands and squeezed hard. "We'll get Faery back."

"I hope so." He grinned crookedly. "It would be a hell of an ending if we had to retreat to the casino for the long haul."

"Eh. Lady Luck isn't so bad. Besides, we wouldn't be there all that long."

"You never told me you inherited your mother's seer gifts."

"I didn't inherit them, but the first lesson of all is visualizing the result you want and never letting go of it. For us, the endpoint is a Faery that's whole again and under your control. Yours and Titania's."

He bent and kissed my forehead before he shimmered out of sight.

I wanted to teleport to Dubrova and get a firsthand look, but Mother shouted for me, and I sprinted to where she hunkered over an injured faun. There'd be time later to survey the castle. For now, my magic was needed here.

15

CHAPTER FIFTEEN, CYN

"Leave. Now," Faery sniped, clearly furious Dariyah had spurned her.

I'd traveled directly to the crystalline cave after leaving Dariyah, Auril, and a phalanx of injured and dying in the glade. Faery could indeed talk with me. After all those years of silence, it was a welcome change.

"I'm not that easy to get rid of," I told her.

"This is your fault."

Oh really? She wanted to play the blame game? Two could ride that horse, but if I jumped on, it would only make a bad situation worse.

"How is it my fault?" I kept my tone mild.

"You left to go after that half-breed spawn of Medusa."

Anger ignited. No one cast disparaging comments

about Dariyah. No one. I swallowed back hot words. "You left too," I pointed out.

"Aye, but I came to my senses and returned."

My heart thrummed loudly. Its beat was obvious, balanced against the silence of the cave. Diplomacy was one thing, but if Faery and I were going to have any kind of liaison, it had to be based on trust. She'd deserted her hold on Dariyah because of Medusa. She knew it. Worse, I knew it, and it sat like a hulking dragon breathing poison between us.

If I addressed it, would I alienate her forever?

The path I chose dodged the issue. For now. "My lady, I have a proposal for you."

"What might that be?"

Hmmm. So far, so good. At least she hadn't told me to get lost again. "Oberon's connection with you is finally broken, but it left a void. You are vulnerable to malicious infiltration."

"I already know as much." Her tone was peevish. I'd never viewed her as petty before, but then I hadn't possessed the link that would have offered me insights into how she functioned.

"My offer is this," I said. "I am willing to swear a blood oath to bind me to it. Allow me to fulfill my pledge as regent to Faery. Part of that pledge is a connection with you. The important element is I will voluntarily withdraw my presence if you request it." She wasn't reacting, so I plowed on. "Oberon refused to release you. You wouldn't run into that problem with me."

"But there is no more Faery," she wailed. "I've been overrun with hostile mages."

"There will always be a Faery," I reassured her. "We may be down, but we're not out. We'll uncover a way to bend this to our advantage, but to do that, I need to claim my rightful link with you. If you refuse me, the King of Winter won't give you a choice."

It surprised me he hadn't already staked a claim to her, but I didn't bring that up. I also didn't mention Pegasus or Medusa on purpose. Faery was probably still smarting from her cowardice. She may have glossed over her flight with lots of excuses, but she'd been afraid. And it didn't sit well.

Silence hung heavy in the crystal cave. I gathered additional inducements that might make Faery more likely to accede. I was just shunting them into a logical order when she said, "I agree. Do your part before I change my mind."

A whoosh of magic slammed into me, and the spot she always should have been was full. The feel of her was intoxicating. I hadn't counted on that part. I'd viewed the land-link as more of a burden. Withdrawing my dirk from its sheath, I cut a short swipe in the ball of my thumb. Droplets oozed into the air and disappeared.

Blood oath offered and received.

My job here was done. I withdrew from the cave. Faery was despondent—and guilt-ridden. I had enough problems in front of me without hanging around and being tainted by her bleak mood. Because I was curious, my first stop was a vantage point where I could get a look at Dubrova. For the first time since I'd been appointed regent, I had both linkages in place: my people and the land.

The brief stint when I couldn't sense Faery's citizenry was over. It added fuel to my working theory Oberon had been stripped of everything. I hoped suffering was the coin of the realm wherever he'd ended up. No amount of agony could compensate for the pain he'd inflicted on a land he was charged to protect, but eternal misery was a strong start.

The castle no longer glowed with an inner light. The pink stones had turned gray. The moat was empty. Thank the gods Ysir had the presence of mind to send the serpents to the sea. The Unseelie had set up camp in the courtyard on both side of the gates surrounding the castle. Their tents and paraphernalia extended to the edges of the forest.

Everything they touched died. The nearest trees had taken on an unhealthy appearance. Leaves and needles fell to the ground. I wanted to reach out, reassure them this was a temporary setback, but revealing my position by deploying magic would be stupid.

I eyed the castle. Could I risk teleporting into my rooms? I was confident no one had entered them. My warding would have held like it always did, a bulwark against thieves and the curious. One thing was certain, if I were going to make a foray to gather my various magical accoutrements, there wouldn't be a better time. As the King of Winter solidified his power base, storming Dubrova would grow more difficult.

Either I did this, or I returned to the Midnight Court. No middle ground. The worst thing that could happen is I'd be apprehended. And then, my bet was they'd pack me off to join Oberon, wherever they'd stashed him.

Think positive or shelve the project an inner voice sniped. *If you're going to do something, do it soon.*

Cataloguing every little thing that could go wrong tempted disaster. I swathed myself in a ward, visualized my suite of rooms, and launched my spell half-expecting it to bounce me halfway back to Earth. When my familiar chamber took shape, no one was more surprised than me. As I'd expected, nothing had been disturbed. Probably not for lack of trying. No ward is bulletproof; they'd drill through the one around my rooms eventually, but the Unseelie had other priorities.

Like solidifying their hold on Faery. The King would

discover soon enough I'd beaten him to the land. He'd be furious, but I'd be gone from Dubrova before that happened. The brief conversation with Medusa on that goddess-forsaken stretch of hellish beach corroborated my fears they planned to suck the life from Faery's bones, and then cast her aside.

I moved quickly, scooping my sensitive magical aids from drawers and cupboards. Once I had a pile in the center of the room, I packaged it up much as I'd done with Dariyah's possessions back on Earth. A last minute addition was the teakwood box where I kept my few jewelry items. Stones hold power. So do precious metals.

Leaving was hard. Who knew if I'd ever return to the castle where I'd spent over a thousand years? Even worse, the battle where Faery was lost had played out while I was gone. I'd been needed here, but my presence on Sarpedon Island had ensured Medusa's exit. Between my sword and the seeds I'd planted about Pegasus being in danger, I'd wagered she'd leave. And she had.

Careful to conceal my presence and my destination, I grabbed the enchanted container with the instruments I'd collected and set a path for the Midnight Court. Auril had nailed it when she said destiny has a way of finding you. Mine had been following Dariyah. Even if I'd been here, it wouldn't have changed the tide of events. Judging from the sheer numbers fanned around the castle, the King of Winter had been planning this for a long while.

My aim was truer than usual, probably because Faery was riding shotgun. The glade bustled with activity. I set my packet of possessions off to one side. Ysir reached me first. "My library. What will happen to my library? There are things that must not fall into enemy hands."

It was news to me. I've always valued learning, but what earthly difference would it make who had their paws on a moldering heap of vellum? I focused my attention on Ysir. "What kind of things?"

He pushed himself straighter amid creaking bones and joints. "The main ones I'm worried about are the scrolls with instructions for how to mix magics. Whoever commands those techniques can make themselves much stronger."

I had a niggling hunch the Unseelie had already dipped their toes into those waters. "What part of the library?" I asked.

He slitted his gaze at me. "Why?"

"You know why," I replied. "Moving shelves worth of materials isn't practical. No way we could get in and out quickly enough to escape notice."

"You can't destroy them." His voice shrilled. Movement rolled around us as people came and went tending to the wounded.

"If you have a better idea, out with it," I said.

He touched me, and I felt a shiver of magic. Wonder creased his face. "You finally are regent in more than name."

"I am. I hold all the necessary linkages." Gripping his forearm, I said, "Can I trust you to do the right thing with your library?"

"Aye, Regent. I shall see to it."

"The Unseelie aren't paying close attention," I told him. "I was just in and out of my rooms, but I wasn't there for more than a handful of minutes."

"Follow your connection to me, and to the castle. You will know when I am finished." Ysir wore a determined look.

"Be exceptionally careful. No matter what method you choose, fire or an earth slide or some other technique, the moment it begins, the Unseelie will notice. You must set the stage and then leave before your casting triggers destruction."

"I understand."

Before I could shower him with a spate of mother hen instructions, he was gone. I felt like a shit. I'd just sent a parent off to murder his children, but the alternative sucked even worse.

Dariyah ran toward me. Her face and hands were streaked with blood. "You're back. Did—?" Her mouth widened into a smile. "You're one with Faery. I can feel it. I was worried she'd hold my refusal against you."

"She almost did, but almost doesn't count." I swept Dariyah into my arms and held her.

She hugged me back. "I can't stay long. We're making progress, but so many are injured."

"Is everyone here?"

"I believe so. Mother did something to draw all Faery's inhabitants to this place. I didn't think they'd fit, but so far it doesn't seem crowded."

Auril must have intuited we were talking about her because she hurried over. "Glad you're back," she told me.

"I made a brief stop in Dubrova for items I couldn't easily replace." I gestured at the ragtag heap of potions, powders, wands, crystals, and my spellbook. "The castle is dying. So are the trees nearest it."

"Is there anything we have to clear out of the castle?" Auril asked.

"I sent Ysir to purge his library of anything the Unseelie might make use of."

"Aw geez." Dariyah detached herself from me. "I bet that will damn near kill him."

"Probably, but he'll do what he has to." I turned to Auril. "Catch me up on this place. Is it infinitely expandable? How will all of Faery fit here? Or will it?"

She sent a curt nod my way and chewed on her lower lip before saying, "When I left the King of Winter I needed a place that still had Faery's magic but was separate enough from her to avoid easy discovery. Faery understood my dilemma and crafted a mirror world. I've never had need for all of it, but it should accommodate everyone."

"Do we need a plan B if it doesn't?" I asked.

"I'm not certain." Auril pushed a hank of hair out of her face. "We're in uncharted territory. While I scryed today's debacle, what comes next was never clear to me."

"There you are." Titania strode briskly in our direction. Her long white hair had fallen out of its braids and hung in tangles around her. She stopped before she reached me and narrowed her eyes.

Before she could stab me with magic, I said, "I am whole. Linked to both land and people, Faery finally has a true regent."

"Marvelous news. Simply marvelous." She closed the distance between us and gripped my hands in hers. "Should make regaining our ascendancy simple enough."

"I'm not so sure of that," Auril told her sister.

Titania flapped a hand her way. "Bosh. What could be easier? Oberon is gone. I can't feel his slimy essence anywhere. All we have to do is..."

I listened to her for a respectful period—after all, she was still queen, while I was merely regent—but then I requested leave to speak.

"Of course, dear lad. Tell them we'll get everyone in tiptop shape and take our castle back. And our land."

"I stopped at Dubrova. At least 10,000 Unseelie are camped in the courtyard and beyond the gates. I've never seen such a large force. Gargoyles and the same twisted beasts we saw earlier walk among them."

The queen's exuberance faded. "What are you saying?"

"We're outnumbered. Badly. Reclaiming what's ours will required planning, stealth, and a healthy shot of luck."

Titania rolled her shoulders back. "We'll get there."

"Aye. We will."

Auril hooked a hand beneath Titania's arm; the two women walked toward groups of Fae and Sidhe who were working over the wounded. A herd of unicorns ambled past, followed by groups of satyrs and nymphs. Birds trilled from overhead, as if their songs could heal the pain from our defeat.

"No one is defeated until they give up," Dariyah said.

I draped an arm around her shoulders. "Not a thought to call my own, huh?"

"Never. Until you tell me to get lost."

"Not going to happen."

She leaned into me, but not for long. "They need my help," she said. "Something about my blend of magics lends itself to healing. Who would have guessed?"

"I'm going to gather Faery's court, assuming

everyone is still alive. We'll have a quick meeting and start planning for the immediate future."

"Good idea. Where will you be later?"

I considered the question and turned it back her way. "Where would you like us to be later?"

Her full mouth curved into a smile. "Dinner at Lady Luck? The food's grown on me. And then, I want to look in on Midnight. When I left, I told him I might not return."

"It was true," I said softly. "Better to prepare him than for him to be forever waiting and wondering. How about the casino at seven tonight?"

"Perfect. Even if I'm not done here, I'll be ready for a break." She tilted her head. "It's welcome, but my power replenishes itself naturally here."

"It would. Faery recognizes her own."

Dariyah began to laugh. "She may forgive me eventually, but right now I'm the last mage on her list to claim."

Turning, I threaded my other arm around her and kissed her. Sweet urgency danced between us, the promise of more than kisses tantalizing but out of reach for the moment.

In the depths of my mind, I heard Faery shouting, *"Not her. Anyone but her."*

I'm not sure if Dariyah heard her, and I ignored the message. Dariyah was mine. I was linked to the land. Even Faery wasn't petty enough to chase me away because of Dariyah. Other options to bond with were nonexistent.

Faery would get over her snit. She had to.

Dariyah broke our kiss, said, "See you later," and ran lightly toward a faun calling her name.

I walked the glade, talking with everyone I could as I offered reassurance and support. Ysir shimmered into corporeality when I was between a herd of unicorns and a bunch of Fae. The aged librarian's cheeks were tear-stained. He said, "It is done," about the time I felt an explosion through my connection to Faery.

My eyes widened. "What did you do?"

"Blew up the castle. It was dying anyway. I just hurried things along."

It was a bold move. Far brasher than anything I'd have done. I clapped Ysir across the shoulders. "Good man."

His thin lips formed a rare smile. "Go big or go home."

Him borrowing modern terminology amused me. "Where'd you hear that one."

"Listening to you young'uns. If I may have your leave, Regent, I'd like some time to myself."

"Certainly. You don't need permission."

"Thank you. I shall think on what's next for me. A librarian needs a library, and I just obliterated mine."

I stood quietly as he walked away with his spine

straight and his head held high. It was as good a time as any to call the court into session. Raising my mind voice, I summoned the delegates and asked them to meet me as soon as they could.

You've reached the end of *Midnight Court*. Keep reading for a teaser chapter from *Court of the Fallen*. Please take a few moments and leave a review for *Midnight Court*. Do it now while it's fresh in your mind. Reviews mean so much to authors, and they're your opportunity to share what you loved about a book with other readers just like you.

BOOK DESCRIPTION: COURT OF THE FALLEN

Urban fantasy and slow burn romance wrapped into a serial that will keep you up reading long into the night.

Strange bedfellows rock worlds.

Faery has changed so much I barely recognize her. I suppose every regent who loses a major war feels the same way about his country. The worst part is I didn't see this coming. A few minor skirmishes, sure, but the Unseelie fielded tens of thousands against us. The King of Winter is finally exacting revenge against the consort who spurned him. The rest of us are collateral damage. He played his hand well, attracted powerful allies, and punted us into a definite one-down position.

For the moment.

Pegasus is the king's primary ally. I possess knowledge that will blow their partnership sky high. And proof in case neither of them believes me. Timing is everything, though. Not putting my evidence in danger is at the tiptop of my list. I love her, and I wouldn't draw attention her way if it weren't necessary. She'd pooh-pooh my pussyfooting around. Even if I wanted to muffle her connection to Pegasus, she'd overrule me and throw it in his horsey face.

We must wrest Faery from the enemy. I finally hold the land link, but success is far from a foregone conclusion. More blood will flow before we're done. Buckets of the stuff, but I can't let it stop me.

COURT OF THE FALLEN,
CHAPTER ONE, TITANIA

Titania ducked into a quiet clearing away from the mass of injured scattered across the verdant glade of the Midnight Court. She needed a break from tending to Faery's assorted inhabitants. Most would recover, but helping a few past their pain was a final kindness. Even though it was the only reasonable path, each death seared her soul. Faery's inhabitants were immortal, but immortality only went so far. It didn't take a crystal ball, or her sister's assorted scrying tools, to know things weren't going especially well.

Being gone from Faery for half a century didn't help anything, but it wasn't as if she'd had a choice in the matter. Titania marshaled her practical side. She was back in Faery, and she aimed to remain there. Her fatal error had been not taking it seriously when her erstwhile consort's troops had shanghaied her. She'd been certain it was one more of his many machinations designed to exert control over her, but when weeks had passed, followed by months, the ugly truth had dawned.

Oberon wasn't coming to release her. No one was.

She'd upped the ante on her escape efforts, but Oberon had clearly planned her abduction and planned it well. No matter what she did, she hadn't been able to break free. Her own magic was part and parcel of her prison, woven into the stuff of the miniature castle holding her captive. When she cut its flow, she effectively crippled her ability to do anything else too.

Almost back in her rightful spot, Titania didn't waste time stewing over trivialities. Dubrova Castle was where she should have been, but Ysir, the ancient Fae librarian, had just blown it sky high to keep the King of Winter and his Unseelie hordes from helping themselves to various castle treasures, including what had been a rich and varied collection of books and scrolls.

The library was an incalculable loss, but she couldn't stop to grieve about collected lore and wisdom that dated to the beginnings of the world.

Thank all the gods Oberon appeared to be out of the way. He'd no doubt outlived his usefulness to the King of Winter, who'd never had any intention of sharing Faery with anyone once it fell under his control.

"There you are." Cynwrigg ap Llyr, regent of Faery, popped into view. With his tall, lithe body, ice-blond hair, and eyes like burnished metal, he was one striking man. Oberon had been beautiful, but Cynwrigg outshone him by a factor of a hundred. Dark trousers clung to his long legs, and a cream-colored linen shirt with old-fashioned bell sleeves cinched at the wrists flowed around his shoulders and torso. Scuffed leather boots graced his feet.

"Here I am." She eyed him and girded herself for whatever he wanted. He'd obviously been hunting for her, which meant he had a purpose in mind.

"I've assembled the court, my queen. By the grace of the gods, all the delegates survived. It would be good for morale if you joined us."

A corner of her mouth twisted into a sneer. "Court of the fallen, eh?"

He slitted his eyes and gripped her forearm. Before she could twist away and rebuke him for touching her, he said, "Our situation is temporary. Snide commentary like that won't help any of us."

She jerked her arm out of his grip. "Now look here. Calling a spade a spade is honest. We have to tack down a starting point to develop plans that have any hope of success."

The stark set to Cynwrigg's features softened slightly. "Every one of Faery's citizens is all too aware we lost the battle despite their best efforts. Most know Ysir leveled Dubrova. The explosion sent shockwaves through the land. Coming up with a label that memorializes our failure isn't helpful."

Anger moved from a simmer to a slow boil. How dare he tell her the right way to treat with her subjects. Hers, not his. "I was queen long before you were born, and—"

"Your point?" he cut her off rudely.

"You could be replaced," she sputtered expecting him to fold.

"All right by me," he shot back. "I never wanted to be regent, and I still don't, but I will uphold my duty to the land and to you." Breath swished from between his teeth. "Come join the court. They can vote someone else into my slot."

"I heard some of that." Auril bustled into the clearing. What had felt like plenty of space for one was growing crowded. Her sister's long, lush red hair hung in tangles to her waist. Smudges of dirt and blood tracked down her face and coated her hands. Silver eyes bored into her and Cynwrigg as she glanced from one to the other of them. Auril had always been tall. Not quite up to Cynwrigg's seven-foot height, but not far from it, either. A dark blue skirt hung off her hips and she wore a black blouse and leather vest with a million little pockets stuffed with healing powders, potions, and crystals. As usual, her feet were bare.

"So you were eavesdropping, so what?" Titania countered.

"Our people are understandably shaken." Auril switched to mind speech. *"We must present a united front and shore them up. If we do not, they won't have the heart for the series of battles I've seen in my pool."*

"I thought you didn't have a clear picture of what comes next," Cynwrigg said.

Auril nodded. "I didn't, but I've taken the odd break here and there and looked. The future has a way of showing itself to me in its own time, and—"

"Do we win?" Titania cut her sister off. She wasn't interested in fluff, only in results.

Auril skewered her with an annoyed expression. "Eventually. If we don't make any more mistakes."

"I wasn't even here," Titania reminded her. "So if there were errors..." She quit talking. She'd just been replaying her serious lapse in judgement not pulling out every weapon in her arsenal to fight off Oberon's henchmen fifty years before. Her statement about none of this being her fault died unspoken.

"If there were errors, what?" Auril asked sweetly.

"Never mind." Titania snapped her jaws shut before she stuffed her foot so far into her mouth a sandal emerged from her ass.

"I'm going to greet the court," Cynwrigg said. "I would very much appreciate both of you being there." Turning on his heel, he left without another word. He'd taken the wind out of her sails with his proclamation he'd be delighted to step down as regent. Since he didn't care about the position, it didn't leave her much leverage. Or any at all.

Auril dropped a hand onto her shoulder. "We're not at our best, none of us," she began.

"Stuff it."

The hand gripping her shoulder tightened almost to the point of pain. "Sister," Auril hissed, "no one is pleased by today's outcome. If we don't get lost squabbling among ourselves, we might pull out of the hole we've dug ourselves into."

Titania straightened her back. "We did not do this to ourselves. We were the victims of a nefarious scheme that trapped us in its maw."

"Wrong answer. We only turn into victims when we feel sorry for ourselves. Goddammit, Titania, draw yourself together. Be Faery's queen, not some simpering ninny running around proclaiming the sky has fallen."

"I resent that." She sent a short blast of magic designed to make Auril let go, but her sister clung like a stubborn limpet. "The sky did fall. Faery is heading into her endgame."

Auril switched things up and drew back a hand. For a

moment she thought her sister was going to slap her. It wouldn't be the first time, but Auril dropped her arm to her side and growled, "Desperate straits, yes. Endgame suggests a point of no return, and we are not out of choices. Not yet. I'm going to join the court. I suggest you get past whatever is eating you up alive and do the same."

Titania stared after her retreating form. Back in the day, no one in Faery would have dared address her in such a manner, sister or no. Oberon had meted out punishment for insubordination and—

"Aye, and he's gone," she muttered. "I was only the queen, the consort. No one took me seriously." Titania swallowed hard. Truth was a bitter draught, but important to face. She had an opportunity to establish herself as Faery's remaining royalty in more than name, and she wouldn't do it with negativity. It didn't matter whose fault today was.

What was critical was what they did about it. When she wasn't so pissed, she'd thank Auril for a timely boot in the butt. For now, she hurried out of the place she'd hoped for a respite—and hadn't found one—to the rows of wounded. Work awaited. She'd do a spot more healing, and then drop in on the court.

A unicorn cantered up to her. "You're needed at the north end of the glade, my queen."

The pair of satyrs she'd been summoned to help both

made it. Auril's daughter, Dariyah, had mixed magics with her, which speeded up the process considerably. The woman was a powerhouse. Titania's understanding of why her sister had heeded the call of fortune and mated with Pegasus came into true focus for the first time. When they'd finished with the satyrs, Dariyah rocked back on her heels and said, "That went well, Auntie."

Titania nodded. "Our enchantments blend nicely."

"They should." Dariyah grinned. "Blood knows its own and all that goes with it. I'm going to clean up and join the court."

"As am I. If anyone asks, tell them I'll be there soon." She hadn't realized those were her intentions until the words slipped out, but she'd wait a few more minutes before leaving the impromptu field hospital. Something about drawing the strands of body and soul back together had a centering effect. After two more healings —and one death—she pushed to her feet and headed to where she assumed Cynwrigg had assembled the court.

Sure enough, they were arranged around the altar Auril used to convene the Midnight Court. Cynwrigg spied her immediately and gestured her forward. As if she required an invitation.

Stop. Just stop. Her caustic inner critic shouted. *Be one with your people. It's the only way.*

After her last interaction with Cynwrigg, he could

just as well have ignored her. Except he wouldn't have done that. He wasn't being polite; he was laying the foundations to restore Faery's confidence. He'd been frank about how he felt about being regent, so he was putting Faery first, above his personal wishes.

If he could manage it, by the goddess so could she.

"Thank you," she said and nodded his way before turning to the dozen court delegates, Ysir, Auril, and Dariyah. The Fae librarian had changed. He no longer looked like a doddering old man. In his place stood a warrior, harsh and resolute.

"The wounded required my presence. It is why I was late," she told the group.

No reason to mention she'd needed time to become the queen they deserved.

"Please. Tell me what ground you've covered," she went on. "What's been decided, and what remains to be hammered out?"

Auril rose to her feet. "Mostly, I've been doing my damnedest to home in on the immediate future."

"You said you'd seen parts of it. What grew clearer?" Titania crooked two fingers her sister's way while marveling once again how much she and Dariyah resembled one another. More like twins than mother and daughter.

"We require assistance. No matter how I spin the

elements, there is no way we can wrest our land back without help."

"Will the dragons be sufficient?" Titania arched a brow.

Auril shook her head. "They might have been if Pegasus and that mother of his weren't involved."

"But they're only two," Titania protested. "Surely we can neutralize them somehow."

"Not only two," Auril corrected her. "That would be simpler. Medusa is one of three Gorgons. Stheno and Euryale are her sisters. Unlike Medusa, they are truly immortal. Medusa had to jump through hoops after Perseus chopped off her head."

"Keep going," Titania urged. She knew Auril well enough to understand there was more.

"Aye. Medusa birthed another monster beyond Pegasus. Chrysaor is a giant, loyal to Pegasus, and very much a power to be reckoned with. And then there are the Shadow Lords. I am not certain of their involvement, but we must ready ourselves in case they play a part of this." Auril pursed her mouth into a sour expression. "There never was anything wrong with the King of Winter's mental capacities. He chose his allies well."

He had, indeed. Titania took in the court delegates. They didn't appear as devastated as she'd figured they would be. "Chrysaor is a winged wild boar if I remember properly."

"Some legends depict him as a mighty warrior wielding a golden blade," Cynwrigg tossed out.

"Not sure it matters," Auril said. "I believe he can select which form he presents. Both are deadly. But it isn't those arrayed against us so much as how their magic slots together. What I'd begun to say was we require intervention from those more powerful than us."

Titania didn't like the sound of that. Auril must be referring to the gods, and they'd never been particularly accommodating. Her only interactions with them had ended up with her retreating, tail between her legs and swearing she'd never put herself in that position again.

Eh. Never is a long time.

"What exactly did your scrying reveal, Sister?"

"It doesn't work that way, and you know as much," Auril replied. "I have seen battles replay themselves many ways, but all with the same ending. We lose again."

"Were dragons fighting alongside us?"

"Aye, they were. It dragged the fighting out, but the results were the same. Three Gorgons and two monsters, a Shadow Lord lurking on the sidelines, plus all those Unseelie were too much. Now if we could send the Unseelie battalions back to wherever they came from—"

"Did we ever figure out where their portal led?" Cynwrigg broke in.

One of the unicorn delegates whinnied. "No. The

dragons did close the gateway, but when we looked more closely, magic bounced back at us."

"They must have a staging area on some other world," Titania said.

"I suggested much the same," Dariyah chimed in. "Even offered to hunt for it."

Titania rolled her shoulders back and wished for her sister's height. Hell, she wished for a lot of things. Her scepter. Her cozy rooms in Dubrova. She had to forget any of them had ever existed.

"I will be forthright with you," she said, "calling in any of the gods is my last choice. Not that we can't do it if nothing else works, but they've never guaranteed much of anything except strife. Getting them to agree on a direction that meshes with our needs would be our first challenge. Even if they did, they'll have their own agendas. And they won't tell us about them until it comes time to pay the piper for their help. We may not care for the price, but by then it will be too late to quibble."

She shrugged. "We could attempt to clarify details at the front end, but if it's in their best interest to keep us in the dark, it's exactly what they'll do."

"Sounds like you've had direct experience," Cynwrigg observed.

"I have." She stopped there, unwilling to vomit up her humiliation at the hands of the gods. Oberon had sent her on several junkets until she'd refused to be his errand girl anymore.

Ysir pushed upright. "If I may, my queen."

"Certainly," she replied.

"The way I see it"—Ysir walked until he stood next to her and Cynwrigg facing the group—"our first task is to locate the place the Unseelie are congregating and destroy it. It won't make a dent in the bunch ranged around what used to be Dubrova, but at least it will cut down on having to deal with more of them.

"While some of us are working on that project, others can research the magic standing against us." His lined face crinkled into a bitter smile. "I made a good show of blowing up the castle, but I preserved most of the library. No one will wade through the wreckage looking for its contents, but that cuts both ways. We will have trouble accessing the materials too."

Titania felt like cheering. Loss of the library had dealt them crippling blow, except it wasn't gone after all.

Cynwrigg clapped Ysir across the shoulders. "You should consider a career on stage. I believed you when you said a librarian needed a library and you'd obliterated yours."

Ysir's smile widened. "'Twasn't too far off the mark. Everything around it was annihilated."

"Good man. Thanks for not following my instructions."

Ysir turned to Cynwrigg. "Not a problem, Regent. It's good you're not wedded to being in charge. Had you been, you might have minded me picking a different road."

"Not at all." Cynwrigg shook his cascade of hair behind his shoulders. "I felt like a bastard sending you off to destroy the history of our people, but the alternative would have been worse."

"I understand. I bought us the best of both worlds. We shall see how things play out."

"Who will search out the Unseelie lair?" Titania projected her voice until she hoped it smacked of command.

"Dariyah and I will take a crack at it," Cynwrigg said.

"And I will creep into the library and gather what I can about the Gorgons, Pegasus, and Chrysaor," Ysir said.

"It's a solid start," Titania said. "Those of us who are here will shore up Faery's citizens. Some will require time before they're fully themselves again. Meanwhile, take the healthy and form companies. Practice battle techniques every day. We didn't start with a country of warriors, but it's no reason why we can't build one."

Cheers rang out, startling her. What she'd said hadn't been all that inspiring. Or maybe it had. She wasn't in a position to judge.

Auril joined her. "Might I add an item or two?"

"Go ahead."

"I will continue to scry our future at every opportunity," Auril told the group. "I will also convene the Midnight Court. It will help us heal." She turned to Titania. "How often would you like us to touch base?"

Titania smothered a grimace. Auril was subtlety reminding her what she'd left out. "Let's get back together two afternoons hence at about this same time. If you miss a meeting or two because you're not here, find me on your return and I can let you know how we're doing as we move forward.

"And we will move forward," she went on. "Faery suffered a monumental loss today, but we are not done for. We will rise above this. We will reclaim our land."

When the shouting and clapping had died down, she turned to Cynwrigg. "Before you leave, check in with the land."

"Aye, my queen. I'd planned to do just that."

"Does anyone have any questions? Ideas? Things we missed today?" Titania let her gaze settle on each delegate in turn. She knew them all, and a more solid bunch of mages didn't exist in all of Faery.

No one said anything, so she went on, "As you go about your tasks, things will come to you. Write them down and bring them to the next meeting."

Amid a sea of yesses and ayes, the group disbanded.

Titania turned to go too, but Auril grabbed her arm. "Nicely done."

She turned to her sister and lowered her voice. "Thanks."

"None needed. You know me. I never lavish praise when it hasn't been earned."

"You're not kidding," Dariyah sniped and then laughed.

Leaving them to make fun of one another, Titania walked toward Auril's modest cottage. Today had gone better than she'd expected. Not only had she instilled hope in the court delegates, she actually believed her own hype. The future wasn't as desperate as she'd painted it.

She was queen of these lands, and she'd see things through, supporting Faery through the bumpy road ahead. Not having to sit in Oberon's shadow and forever worry about his moods was an incredible boon. She'd make mistakes, but she'd recover from them.

"Aye," she murmured half to herself, "a queen who never blunders isn't doing enough, isn't taking chances, isn't being the best possible leader for her people."

She passed beneath the lintel of Auril's home and poured herself a tumblerful of mead, sighing as the spicy heat of it passed down her throat. She'd earned an hour or two to herself, but then she'd be back in the thick of things.

"Sister." Auril's telepathy held sharp edges. *"You're needed now."*

Titania drained the rest of her glass. Maybe it was a good thing she hadn't sat down. *"Where?"*

"The eastern border of the Midnight Court. We caught two Unseelie, and—"

"Interrogate them," Titania ordered.

"Too late. They're dead, but this means they've found us."

"Maybe. Maybe not. On my way."

She bolted from the house and took off running. It was almost as fast as a teleport spell, and the movement helped clear her mind. It was possible the Unseelie hadn't yet reported in. It was also possible they'd wandered into Auril's lands accidentally. The Midnight Court cast a seductive allure, drawing all things magical.

She'd issue blanket orders that all spies were to be tortured until they talked. It was messier than killing outright, but war was messy business. Brutalizing the Unseelie held a certain appeal. More than an appeal. She was looking forward to jabbing and prodding and cutting off body parts.

The coppery smell of fresh blood made her alter course. She bounded into a thicket and found Auril, a unicorn, and a couple of nymphs standing over the corpses. "Cut off their right hands and have the birds drop them into the middle of the Unseelie camp."

Auril grinned. "Why, Sister. What a splendid idea."

"Forcing them to talk would have been even more 'splendid,'" she retorted.

"Agreed." The unicorn pawed the ground. "I gored them. Next time, I shall exercise restraint."

She patted his flank. "I know you will. Get to it."

ABOUT THE AUTHOR

Ann Gimpel is a USA Today bestselling author. A life-long aficionado of the unusual, she began writing speculative fiction a few years ago. Since then her short fiction has appeared in many webzines and anthologies. Her longer books run the gamut from urban fantasy to paranormal romance. Once upon a time, she nurtured clients. Now she nurtures dark, gritty fantasy stories that push hard against reality. When she's not writing, she's in the backcountry getting down and dirty with her camera. She's published over 85 books to date, with several more planned for 2020 and beyond. A husband, grown children, grandchildren, and wolf hybrids round out her family.

Keep up with her at www.anngimpel.com or http://anngimpel.blogspot.com

If you enjoyed what you read, get in line for special offers and pre-release special reads. Newsletter Signup!

Blood and Sorcery

Blood and Illusion

Demon Assassins

Witch's Bounty

Witch's Bane

Witches Rule

Dragon Heir

Dragon's Call

Dragon's Blood

Dragon's Heir

Dragon Lore

Highland Secrets

To Love a Highland Dragon

Dragon Maid

Dragon's Dare

Dragon Fury

Earth Reclaimed

Earth's Requiem

Earth's Blood

Earth's Hope

Elemental Witch

Timespell

Time's Curse

Time's Hostage

Gatekeeper

Shadow Reaper

Rebel Reaper

Untamed Reaper

GenTech Rebellion

Winning Glory

Honor Bound

Claiming Charity

Loving Hope

Keeping Faith

Ice Dragon

Feral Ice

Cursed Ice

Primal Ice

Magick and Misfits (Fall and Winter 2020)

Court of Rogues

Midnight Court

Court of the Fallen

Court of Destiny

Rubicon International

Garen

Lars

Soul Dance

Tarnished Beginnings

Tarnished Legacy

Tarnished Prophecy

Tarnished Journey

Soul Storm

Dark Prophecy

Dark Pursuit

Dark Promise

Underground Heat

Roman's Gold

Wolf Born

Blood Bond

Wolf Clan Shifters

Alice's Alphas

Megan's Mates

Sophie's Shifters

Wylde Magick

Gemstone

Lion's Lair

Unbalanced

STANDALONE BOOKS

Branded, That Old Black Magic Romance (paranormal romance)

Edge of Night (short story collection, paranormal and horror)

Grit is a 4-Letter Word (nonfiction)

Heart's Flame (post-apocalyptic romance)

Icy Passage (science fiction romance)

Marked by Fortune (post-apocalyptic coming of age story)

Melis's Gambit (historical paranormal romance)

Midnight Magic (paranormal romance)

Red Dawn (post-apocalyptic paranormal romance)

Shadow Play (historical paranormal romance)

Shadows in Time (Highland time travel romance)

Since We Fell (contemporary romance)

Warin's War (paranormal romance)